Coloma Woods

By
William Clark

The moral right of the author has been asserted.

The characters and events portrayed in this book are fictitious. Any similarity to real person, living or dead, is coincidental and not intended by the author.

All Who Wander Are Not Lost.

The Beginning

He had heard the sound several times just as he was getting into bed on consecutive nights, heard it enough times in a row to bring up unease about going to sleep in that room alone. It was the kind of intermittent sound that announced a certain level of intelligence behind it, like someone working with metal tools a long way off in the dark, someone or something that wouldn't normally be up that late moving around.

This was the fourth night he had heard it. He was now keeping track of the time it started which was usually around one in the morning. On this night he decided to brave the cold room, very different than the warmth of his bed, and look out the second story window. His room looked over a large back yard and a tall, thick wood-line, a heavy stand of trees that went for a solid hundred acres south of his property.

He leaned towards the open window, close enough to smell the screen. There it was again, a digging sound, no, more like heavy boards being moved, stacked. "What the hell?" he whispered to himself as the muted sounds continued. After several minutes of listening and still not being able to figure out what was causing the noise, he decided to get dressed, grab his pistol, go outside, and see what was going on.

Moving through the dark of his room, he found his pants, socks, and shirt before remembering that he had taken his boots off in his wife's room across the hall. They had been sleeping apart due to his late night work and her penchant for getting up and down all night to use the bathroom or whatever else she decided to do. They had both been using the excuses of work and weak bladders for months now, knowing full well that the excuses were lies. Honestly, they both just got a better night's sleep when they slept in separate beds. Having been married north of ten years, the visceral excitement of sleeping with a woman or man had long since worn off. Now, comfortable in each others company, all they wanted was a good night's sleep. He got dressed and, as quietly as he could, crept across the hall to Sharon's room. Slowly stepping inside, he could hear the deep methodical breathing of someone in sound, heavy sleep.

He found his boots in the closet and slowly crept back out of the room, quietly closing the door behind him. On the way downstairs he picked up his forty-five from the nightstand, ejected the magazine, and then snapped it back in, making sure it was fully loaded. He found his only working flashlight in the catchall drawer in the kitchen and then quietly stepped out the back door and onto the deck.

He shivered from the late-night chill as he stood quietly listening to the night sounds. There it was again, that odd thumping, digging sound coming from somewhere in the dark woods. He strained to hear, trying to get a fix on what direction the sound was coming from. He slowly stepped off the porch and walked across the dew soaked grass, right to the edge of the wood line that started at the back of his property. He hadn't walked thirty yards and already his shoes were soaked. He stopped at the end of the path that meandered into the woods, trying to think of what he should do next.

Shivering more from adrenalin than cold, he stood, weapon and flashlight in hand, working up the courage to head further into the dark. There it was again, that sound. "Son of a bitch," he whispered. What was going on out there? He snapped the weapon off 'safe' and started down the path. This should be interesting.

Chapter One

Preston Dale had been in a funk for days, weeks actually. A pervasive dullness had shaded his days and agitated his nights as he had tried to understand just what it was that had been bugging him. He had turned sixty-three last Tuesday, a milestone in his mind of depressing reality. In youth, he had been a fairly good athlete, never a star, but good enough at most of the ball-sports to contribute to the team. He could hit an inside fastball, catch a well-thrown football, and hit a pretty good jump-shot from the paint. But now, at this age, he doubted that he could even hit a slow-pitch softball. Maybe that was it. Maybe it was the sudden realization that the heavy footfalls of debilitating age were closing fast. Social Security, Medicare, and Senior Citizen discounts at every place he spent money seemed to be all he and his wife, Sharon, had discussed lately.

Old people shit, he thought heading down the basement stairs. That was stuff people talked about during the backside of life, when all the colors and the lights just weren't that bright anymore. Hell, he thought, turning on his basement shop light. He could not remember when he even had had a decent erection, one of those rock-hard, hard-to-walk kind of deals that guys in their prime get. That in itself was enough to make a guy want to jump off a bridge.

He gently touched the paint on the birdhouse to see if the last coat had dried. "Still tacky" he mumbled out loud. That was another thing he had started doing lately, he thought, talking out-loud when he was by himself. Throughout his life he had seen *old people* doing it in supermarkets, on street corners, and in city parks. Now, much to his chagrin, he was doing it. And bird houses…he was now making bird houses just like many other bored senior citizens with way too much time on their hands.

For years he had tried the volunteer route - Lions, Elks, Kiwanis, the standard white-shoes-and-belt crowd, and found it lacking. He had tried the fraternal brotherhood course - Masons, Odd Fellows, Knights of Columbus, and again found that he really did not fit in with those kind of people. Most of the men he had met were either far older or far younger than he and had exuded a weird type of hyper-friendliness that he found disturbing, if not downright annoying. The over-the-top handshake and heavy pat on the back at these gatherings always seemed forced, almost like they were obligated to be 'all teeth and smiles' by the secret shot callers. On top of the weird chumminess, it was compulsory that you had to do things for membership, things he would never have done on his own, things like pancake feeds and mindless social dinners where he would be required to stand behind a table of metal serving dishes, wearing a funny hat and ladling out plates of food to strangers. No, it was not what he had wanted to do on his Thursday nights.

He had lived in the small Michigan town for ten years now and still barely knew his neighbors. Most of it was his fault, not having much in common with the locals, a group of middle-class suburbanites absolutely fascinated with lawn fertilizer, flowerbeds, and crab grass, subjects he found mind-numbingly boring. He smiled when he thought of the time one of his neighbors asked him about his yard and what he planned to do with it come springtime. Without missing a beat, he had told the guy that he planned to pave it with concrete and maybe paint it green. The neighbor, who made love to his yard constantly, smiled uncomfortably and asked if he was serious. "Absolutely," he had replied keeping an even stare. "A manicured lawn is an ironclad sign of insanity. People who engage in that kind of behavior need to be locked up." Needless to say, he hadn't been asked about his yard anymore.

One thing he did like about the people he lived close to was that they kept to themselves. That was just the way he liked it. The word had quickly gotten around that the guy who didn't rake the leaves that fell in October until May was really not into small talk about lawn care.

The town itself was within spitting distance of Lake Michigan, a small Midwestern burg of three thousand, a blistering cold place in the winter, but a nice spot to live weather-wise the rest of the year. The town's claim to fame was that it was once the wooden shingle capital of the Midwest, during the late 1800's. Now it was just another small town, ninety miles from Chicago, a town no one outside a two hundred mile radius had ever heard of.

He had moved to Coloma from Ohio with Sharon in hopes of fulfilling his dream of being a professional writer, having accepted a stringer position at the local paper in town. Over the last several years he had started to sell some of his short stories and had written a short novel that brought in a few hundred bucks a month but nothing like he thought he could make. It seemed the dream was well on its way to dying. In reality they were just barely surviving on his Social Security and Sharon's paycheck. She was selling commercial real estate for a large broker out of Saint Joseph and had been moderately successful, enough to pay the mortgage and keep the lights on.

Last February he had been let go from the paper. Management rolled out the well-worn work termination cliché of corporate downsizing. The notice had been safe, non confrontational, almost clinical, but he knew better. Over the past two years the articles he had written had started to get negative attention from the heavy hitters in the community. Topics had ranged from crooked land development deals to the type of school board scandals that every small town in the country goes through. The work had given him the reputation of a ball buster, someone who was able to light some pretty embarrassing fires the elite didn't care for. He had generated way too much heat, giving management the motivation to show him the door. It was not as if he hadn't seen it coming. He knew full well that reporting on small town business and politics included a lot of dangerous baggage. The town shot callers preferred that their baggage stay in the "*neighborhood,*" as they liked to say, and no cranky outsider would be allowed to dump too much of that pot out onto the street.

Now that his caustic exposés had been dealt with, he spent most of his time writing his novel about World War One and building birdhouses. As he painted on the last coat of varnish, he remembered what a strange sense of relief he had felt when he came home from his last day at the office. Even though he knew the biweekly paychecks would stop coming, at least until he could find something else, he had felt at peace with how he had conducted himself as a professional writer. As brief as it was, he had told the truth. He stood by every word he said, and if asked, he wouldn't have changed a thing. At his age, it was more important than ever to stand for something even if it was unpopular. In his mind the world had turned upside down with a cancerous political correctness, a forced cultural diversity that did nothing but separate people further, and a set of horrific situational ethics from the government down. It was truly amazing how much the country had fallen apart.

****

To the casual observer, the old man in the shabby clothing slowly pushing his cart down the supermarket aisle looked like any other poor, somewhat befuddled senior citizen trying to figure out how to stretch his Social Security money for groceries. His hair was snow white, yet his skin was deeply tanned, like someone who had worked every day outdoors. He walked with a slight limp on his left side, indicating a foot or hip injury, something not uncommon to a man of his age. One of the odd things about the man's appearance was the long, dark brown duster he wore. It was a below the knee length coat, the kind that movie cowboys wore. His shoes were old and battered work boots, footwear that had seen far better days. Yet, with all the worn out clothing and halting gait, the old man's pale blue eyes were clear and focused, his deep-set expression and hooked nose giving him the appearance of a bird of prey.

He slowly walked up beside the sliced meat display and carefully looked over the selection, ham, honey-cooked ham, slow-roasted ham, thin slice and thick slice. "Jesus," he whispered out loud. *Was it so god-dammed hard to just get a package of normal hog meat?* He snatched one of the packages off the hook and quickly stuffed it into the large inside pocket of his coat. He looked around the brightly lit store, hoping no one had seen the theft. Confident that he was in the clear, he slowly moved over to the bread racks and snatched a small loaf of Rye.

He didn't need much, not as much as he used to. Besides, it was hard carrying a lot of weight when he had to get off the ground. He needed three running steps, and since the last injury, his run had turned into a disjointed shuffle - downright embarrassing compared to how he used to be.

This was always the toughest part about his day - getting away without being seen. Years ago he wasn't afraid of confrontation. Now, time and injury had changed his attitude. A man in his eighties didn't need to be fighting anybody. He would get what he needed and then leave the same way he came in. Heading for the automatic front doors, he got careless when he quickly picked up a small jar of mustard off the shelf. As he stuffed it into his pocket, a teenage shelf stocker, who was kneeling down beside several boxes of salad dressing, spoke up. "Sir, sir, you need to pay for that," the kid announced standing. The old man kept walking.

"Sir, you need to pay for that," shouted the kid, walking after the man.

"Shit," whispered the old man as he reached into his coat pocket and pulled out a large coin that hung from a thick silver chain. He didn't like to do it this way, but the kid behind him and the now alerted store manager in front of him gave him no choice.

"Hold on, Sir," announced the older store manager, stepping in front of the old man. "Do we have a problem here?"

"Not anymore, Sonny," replied the old man, draping the chain around his neck and instantly vanishing.

The old man stood still for a second watching the now-stunned store manager stand open mouthed, frozen as if hit with a huge electrical charge.

"Son of a bitch!" shouted the kid running up. "Did you see that shit?"

The store manager, unable to get his mind wrapped around what he had just seen, slowly raised his arm desperately trying to feel the man who had just been there. "Wha, where, where did he go? He just disappeared. He just vanished."

The kid was now on the verge of tears. "Oh my God, oh my God, that was the craziest shit I have ever seen. Unreal!" He shouted, now waving his arms.

The old man slowly sidestepped the two and made his way to the automatic doors. This was always the trickiest part. The sensors would not register him trying to get through so he would have to wait for someone to come in from outside. Seconds later a woman and a small child walked in, leaving him a clear avenue of escape. He stepped outside as the two store employees continued to shout and jump around inside, convinced they had seen some sort of miracle. "Idiots," he mumbled to himself as he made his way across the parking lot.

Years ago it had been fun to put the yips in people with this kind of stunt. But now all he wanted to do was eat, put his feet up, and take a nap. Once he had carefully crossed the main road and made it into the thick woods towards his camp, he lifted the chain from around his neck and put it back into his pocket. Yeah, there had been a day when he would have sought out that kind of encounter. Causing fear of the unknown was addictive. It had made him feel powerful. Now, he just wanted to be left alone. It was amazing what a lifetime of self-induced solitary confinement could do to a man.

Chapter Two

It was a lot harder moving down the path in the dark than he thought it would be. Roots, stumps, and sticker-vines filled the narrow trail making it difficult to walk even with a flashlight. He immediately began questioning the sanity of getting out of a warm bed to stumble around in the dark of the woods as the wind picked up, dropping the temperature even further.

He worked at controlling his natural fear of the night. His imagination, now at full tilt, gave him images of red-eyed creatures and dark slithering things at every turn. Several times, as low hanging tree branches brushed his face or snagged his clothing, a bolt of fear flashed through his body nearly making him pull the trigger of the forty-five in panic.

Finally, he stood in the dark at a wider, smoother part of the trail and worked to get his breathing under control so he could listen to the night sounds and the wind rustling through the trees. Then he heard the sound again, not too far away. It was a chopping sound, like someone cutting wood. He ducked low and crept forward, his pistol at the ready. Rounding a curve several yards further, he spotted the faint orange glow of a campfire.

As he cautiously stepped closer, he could see an old man sitting by the fire, illuminated in the glow. He appeared to be tending a small pot next to the flame. A hobo, thought Preston as he watched the man. So this was the source of the noise that had bothered him for the last week - some old guy living out here in the woods. Not wanting to confront the man, he slowly backed away.

"Something I can do for you?" announced the man sitting next to the fire.

Startled that he had been seen, Preston froze in the shadows, not sure what to do or say. "Ah, no, I'm fine. Sorry to have bothered you," he replied weakly. *Jesus, I sound like such a wimp.*

"You're not bothering me. Awfully late to be out in the woods, isn't it?"

Swallowing his fear, he stuck the pistol in his back pocket and slowly stepped from the shadows. "I could say the same thing about you."

The old man chuckled while poking the fire with a small stick. "Yeah, I guess you're right. You're welcome to come on over. I have coffee on."

"You're camping out here?" asked Preston, not sure what else to say.

The old man looked up at the sky and then back at the fire, smiling. "Yes, sir, I guess you could call this camping. Why don't you have a seat, seeing that you've come this far."

Preston stepped into the small camp, watching the old man closely. The old man looked to be in his eighties with snow-white hair and deep set eyes that were barely visible in the flickering firelight. "You've been out here about a week. Right?"

"That's about right. Am I on your property? If I am, I'll move. Don't want to cause any trouble."

Preston sat down on a short stump across from the man. "No, this is State ground. It's part of a State of Michigan Bird Preserve. My house is right at the edge of it, back there."

The old man kept quiet a moment while staring into the fire. "Michigan is a pretty place," he said quietly. "I like it here." He looked up, his blue eyes catching the light. "My name is Darcy Robashaw. I'd get up and shake your hand but my leg has just about played out."

Preston noticed that the man had his left leg resting on a small log. "Don't worry about it. Are you hurt? Oh, and, I'm Preston, Preston Dale. Pleased to meet you."

"Pleased to meet you." He shifted the weight off his left hip, grimacing from the effort.

"Do we need to get you medical help? How bad are you hurt?" questioned Preston, concerned.

"No, I can get through it. Been hurt far worse than this. I'm thinking I might have twisted something in my ankle."

Preston could now see that the man was in a great deal of pain. "You know, I really do think we need to get you some help. I don't think someone your age should be out here sleeping on the ground."

Darcy chuckled. "My age, huh?" He pushed another stick in the fire, and his dark eyes fixed on a memory. "How old you do you think I am there, Preston?"

"Well, I don't want to offend you, but I'd say you were in your eighties."

"Pretty good guess. I'm eighty-four. Besides this leg being busted, I'm as fit as a fiddle."

Preston stood up. "Jesus, Mister Robashaw, you think it's broken? You know, I really do think we need to get you some help. I'm going to head back to the house and make the call."

Robashaw smiled. "Suit yourself there, Preston. As bad as this leg hurts, I am in no condition to argue with you. I'm just going to sit right here."

****

It took the EMTs a solid hour to get Robashaw out of the woods and into the back of the ambulance later that night. Just before the doors closed he called out to Preston who was standing in the driveway, along with several curious neighbors who had been watching the entire operation.

"They're gonna take good care of you, Mister Robashaw," Preston announced as he stepped up to the back of the brightly lit ambulance.

The old man leaned up on one elbow and tossed a small leather knapsack on the floor. "Preston, would you mind hanging onto that bag for me? I know you don't owe me nothing and I'm a stranger, but I am really nervous about it getting stolen at the hospital." He nodded to the bag and laid back on the stretcher, the pain etched deep in his face.

"Well, I guess. Yeah... okay. What do you have in here anyway?"

"Sir, we need to get rolling," announced the EMT taking Robashaw's vitals. "His color isn't that good, and he's clearly dehydrated. We'll be headed over to the hospital in Watervliet." He reached over and quickly closed the door.

"Mister Robashaw, I'll hold onto your bag for you," shouted Preston holding it up to the back window of the ambulance as it pulled away.

"Why would you agree to keep that old man's bag?" questioned Sharon, stepping up beside him. "And what in God's name were you doing down in the woods this time of night anyway? Are you getting senile?"

Preston put his arm around her shoulders and pulled her close. He could feel her shivering from the night air. He had to admit - she looked pretty cute wearing her pink bathrobe and fuzzy slippers out here in the driveway. "C'mon, Sweetie. Let's go to bed. We'll talk later."

As they walked up the driveway to the house, Preston had a strange feeling that things in his life were about to change. It wasn't so much a premonition, but an unsettled feeling of controlled dread. It was like the fear one has just before a sky dive - that odd mixture of feelings that something big and scary is about to happen and that it is all your own doing. Something was in the wind that night, blowing through the trees. He felt it the moment he had stepped into the old man's camp. He sensed that things would never be the same after this.

****

The doctors at the Watervliet hospital had never seen a man of Robashaw's age with so many healed fractured bones. It was amazing he could still get around considering the amount of injury he had obviously sustained over the years. Because he carried no identification or insurance, his status was classified as indigent. That meant the county would eat the medical costs, a burden the hospital administers would want to be cleared of as soon as possible. As far as Robashaw was concerned, that discharge could not come soon enough. Having lived most of the last thirty years outside, he hated being confined indoors. When asked by the medical staff about his numerous injuries he had remained vague. He made up occupations that might seem plausible, considering the injuries....a rodeo clown, a stuntman, a north woods logger...all deflections, all lies. The truth would have been impossible to fathom.

On his last visit to the room, the doctor told him that he had sustained a fractured ankle and some badly bruised ribs. He would be in the cast and on crutches for a minimum of six weeks. The doctor asked if he had a place to go where he could heal.

Robashaw thought for a moment. "I have a camp."

The doctor was surprised. "What kind of camp? Where?"

Robashaw adjusted the heavy cast on the bed before answering. This is when things got complicated…somebody with an official status was starting to dig into his life and how he lived it. "I, ah, I have a camp set up out behind the Dale property in Coloma. Nice people." It was a lie, of course, but the answer seemed to satisfy the intern who only nodded while writing discharge information on the chart.

"Okay. Sir, I am discharging you this afternoon. Here are your release forms and some other information for follow up appointments. Instructions are included on how I want you to take care of your ankle, as we discussed."

Robashaw took the forms, relieved that he was going to be able to leave without any lengthy explanations or discussions about his life style. He just needed to get out of this bed and outside into the fresh air. He now had a stunning headache that he chalked up to the pervasive antiseptic smell that is generic to every hospital he had ever been in. To Robashaw, it was the odor of death and decay. The doctor handed him the rest of the forms, gave him a hurried smile, handshake and left the room. He had done his part.

Alone in the room, Robashaw dropped the forms into the small trashcan by the bed and slowly swung his cast-laden leg over. He intended to be out of this stupid hospital gown and dressed before that pretty little nurse came back in to wheel him out of here, he thought, grunting from the effort to move. She had helped him get his clothes off when he came in, and he was determined to not repeat that humiliation. In his mind, it just wasn't right for a young girl like that to see him naked…just wasn't proper.

Slowly, he slid off the side of the bed to stand on his good leg. He was surprised by how clumsy he had suddenly become. His arms and hands seemed disjointed and nonresponsive to even the most basic of movement commands. His vision was now starting to grow grey as he fumbled for the rail at the edge of the other empty bed in the room. He could feel himself falling, yet was powerless to stop it. A cool darkness folded in around him and then a total lack of sound except that of his own breathing…a breath….and then another …and then… nothing at all.

Chapter Three

It had been three nights since Preston had ventured into the woods and found the old man with the broken leg. As he stood at his living room window sipping his morning coffee and watching the squirrels jump and run through the leaves of his front yard, he decided that he needed to find out what had happened to him. He punched in the hospital's phone number. "Yes, this is Preston Dale over in Coloma. Ah, three days ago an ambulance picked up an old guy with an injured leg from the back of my place, and he was transported to your hospital. I'm calling to check up on him."

"Are you a relative, sir?"

"Ah, well, no. He was picked up right behind my house; I don't think he has family in the area."

"I'm sorry, sir. I can't give you any information about a patient if you're not a relative."

Preston thought for a moment. "Okay, can you at least give me his room so I can talk to him? Surely you can do that?"

"The name again, please?"

"Ah, he said his name was Darcy... yeah, Darcy Robashaw."

"Just a minute, sir." As Preston waited on hold, he tried to think of what he would say to the old man. He barely knew him and making small talk might be difficult. Plus, he really did not want to become involved with some homeless guy. There was no telling where that could end up going.

"Yes, Mister Dale?"

"I'm here."

"Mister Dale, Mister Robashaw is no longer at this hospital."

"I don't understand. He checked out? Already?"

There was a pause on the phone. "Ah, Mister Robashaw died this morning. His body has been taken to the county morgue. I have a transfer case number if you would like to call them. Is there anything else I can do for you, sir?"

Preston was shocked. "Ah, that's really surprising. I mean he looked okay. Can you tell me what he died of?"

"It says here it was a stroke."

"A stroke? How can he have a stroke from a broken leg? I don't understand."

"Sir, I only have what's written on the release. If you want any more information, you will have to contact the doctor who treated him. And that would be Doctor Nees."

"Ah, well, okay, I guess. Thank you for your help." He disconnected the call, stunned by the news of Robashaw's death. Strange that he felt so bothered by the death of someone he barely knew. Did he have family or someone who cared about him, someone who would want to know that he died camping out in a backwater Michigan bird preserve? There had to be more to the story. He left his easy chair and walked over to where he had put Robashaw's knapsack. Moving things off the kitchen table, he opened the bag and began spreading the contents. Inside, he found a thick, diary-style notebook stuffed full of folded papers, a large hunting knife in a sheath, some hard candy, several pairs of socks with the price tags still on them, a handheld GPS, and a blue velvet Royal Crown whisky bottle bag.

Inside the bag he found a thick roll of twenty-dollar bills tied with a rubber band about two inches across. Also in the bag were two medallions with chains. The two nearly identical medallions were about the size of Olympic medals and were heavy. One was a burnished gold in color, almost a bronze. The other was polished silver. The silver chains that secured the medals were the strongest jewelry wire he had ever seen. The chains were almost as heavy as the medallions themselves. As he looked closely at the medals, he could see that the gold medallion had an inscribed design of a large crane in full flight on one side and the picture of a hawk or eagle also in full flight on the other side. The silver medallion had what appeared to be open castle gates on one side and an etching of a rider-less horse on the other. The writing that had been engraved around the edges of both medals appeared to be some type of Asian script, unlike anything he had ever seen before. But it reminded him of the elfish writing he had seen in the movie "Lord of the Rings." It was very stylish carrying a certain indefinable strength. Sitting back in his chair, he intuitively knew that he was looking at something of great importance, something that was about to change his life forever.

He dropped the medals back into the bag, put the money into his pocket, and then opened the heavily worn notebook. Unfolding the papers, he discovered that there were many different types of court and legal papers. The first one that caught his eye appeared to be a death certificate. The deceased was a *Mrs. Abigail Marie Robashaw of Hamilton, Montana, date of birth October 8, 1929, and date of death June 23, 1999.* Among the papers were a house deed, also in Montana, various vehicle registrations, several insurance certificates, and a complex hand-drawn map of the United States. The map had hundreds of circled spots spanning from coast to coast that were labeled with GPS coordinates. He set the map and papers aside, opened the diary, and began to read the handwriting that filled page after page. Each entry appeared to be titled by date and location.

He began to read one of the entries:

Aug 15, 2001 - Wichita Falls, Kansas.

Landed at around 6:30 at night, nice field, very hot, no wind, went to the local Safeway, picked up some food and batteries. Decided to get a hotel room, need a shower, stayed at the Motel 6 on the highway, decided not to put a cache nearby, way too much construction and development. Stayed two days, left at 3 am on the 17th. Good weather. No problems…

He thumbed through dozens and dozens of similar entries, becoming more intrigued by the minute. All the entries talked of landings and referenced weather in relation to some kind of flight, yet there were no pictures or anything else written into the text that would indicate any particular kind of aircraft that he had been using. Flipping through the pages he came across one of the first entries. It was dated July of 2000, and it literally made the hair stand up on the back of his neck.

July 14, 2000

Went to Crook Shank's auction in Hamilton at 7:00. I bought a weather vein and the box with the Medals. They are very unusual.

He flipped to the second entry, feeling more excited by the second.

July 18th, 2000

Did some research on the medals at the University library in Missoula. The medallions are at least a thousand years old and were cast by Heptereon craftsman, well before the Middle Ages. Professor Grimes said they were VERY valuable and should be in a museum.

Turning to the next page and reading the entry, literally made him stand up from his chair. He could not believe what he had just read.

July 23, 2000

Went to Hamilton to buy groceries. I was in my truck in the Save Mart parking lot and had decided to take one of the medals with me, the silver one, because I like the way it looks. Walking across the lot I put the medal around my neck. Walking up to the large glass doors, I noticed that my reflection could not be seen in the glass, nor would the doors open. Shocked, I stood there for some time until Mrs. Sanders from church walked up. I said hello. She shrieked and nearly passed out right there by the door. Poor woman! She could not see me nor could anyone else who ran up to help her. I had disappeared. I could see myself but to anyone else I was invisible…. As I write these words I still cannot believe it…What does this mean? Maybe I should talk to the Pastor…

He slowly sat back down trying to get his head around what he had just read. These had to be the writings of someone who was seriously unbalanced, yet there was sincerity about the entries. They seemed heart-felt, sane, for lack of a better word. Carefully he picked up the velvet bag and slowly pulled the medallions out. Feeling somewhat foolish, he looked around his empty kitchen, embarrassed by what he was about to do. Not sure what to expect, he slipped the chain over his head letting the medal fall heavily over his heart. He looked at his hands and arms... nothing, nothing had changed. They were still very much visible. He then remembered what Robashaw's last entry had said about not being able to recognize that he could not be seen. A sudden chill ran down his back as he slowly pushed himself out of his chair and made his way toward a large mirror above the fireplace in the living room. This would put an end to this fantasy, this nonsense. He crept across the living room, nearly holding his breath in anticipation, knowing full well that he was being foolish and..."Holy shit!" he shouted out loud, rushing up close to the large mirror. He felt weak in the knees and light headed as he stared at the glass in shocked amazement. He was not dreaming, he was not drunk, and he was not high. He was fucking invisible!

Chapter Four

Sharon had no idea of the life changing events that had taken place at her home while she had been at work. Preston had not made his customary calls to her today and when she rang his cell several times throughout the day, she hadn't gotten an answer. It was strange but not something she had been too alarmed about.

Over the last two years she had settled into the role of a solid performer at work, someone willing to put in the time and effort to move up the food chain. The shot-callers in her organization had noticed and were starting to give her the kind of work she enjoyed. She was thriving in the new responsibilities. Predictability, there was a new corporate buzz attached to her name in the high office meetings and the six o'clock cocktail gatherings. A rumor was floating that the head office for corporate acquisitions out of Atlanta had caught wind of her ability, and that could mean a move east. It was a rumor she hadn't shared with Preston. There was no need spinning everything up before anything official came down the pipe. She knew he had enough on his plate without having to worry about a possible move.

Things in Coloma had not worked out like he had planned when the writing job at the paper had ended in a bad way. She had seen it coming, had bit her lip at the way he was going after certain corrupt community dealmakers in his stories. She had worked in the blood sport world of corporate long enough to know that no matter how good you are at your job, if you piss off the right people at the wrong time, they will take you down. Even a snakehead that's been chopped off its body can still bite. Preston had learned this lesson the hard way, and he now built birdhouses. Old Michigan money has power no matter where the money comes from.

As she pulled off the freeway, a light, early fall rain began to fall. She loved this time of year. The changing leaves, the cool temperatures, and the smell of wood smoke in the air made living in this part of Michigan deeply satisfying. She liked the fact that the winters were hard here. For the locals, it was something to endure, but to her it bonded individuals of the community, those who stuck it out till spring. Nothing is free in life and, in south central Michigan you started paying for the good weather of June around early November. By January the hammer really came down.

Sharon noticed Preston in the front yard as she pulled into the driveway. Walking up to her car, she noticed that he had the strangest look on his face, a combination of excitement and dread, like he now knew some great, yet highly dangerous secret. She wasn't far off. He opened the car door, and before she could get out, he leaned in. "I have to show you something," he announced, his tone barely controlled.

"Okay, Honey, but let me get my folders and purse out of…."

"No time. Let's GO. Leave it," he said, leading her quickly up the sidewalk.

"Preston, stop!" she shouted pulling her hand back. "I need my purse, and I can't leave those contracts in the car. Just wait a second. Geez!"

He grabbed her arm hard as she turned to walk back to the car. "This cannot wait."

She pulled free angrily. It had been a long, tough day, and the last thing she needed now was to have him demanding her time and energy. She just wanted a little peace, a glass of wine, and to not have to deal with any of his drama at the moment. "Preston, just give me a little space, will you please? I have a really bad headache, and I just want a little quiet time, okay? I'll go get my purse and then…"

Without saying a word, he took one step back, pulled a strange looking medallion and chain from his pocket, hung it around his neck and instantly vanished. "Now, do I have you full attention, Sharon!"

At that moment, that second, everything she thought she knew about life and all its wonder evaporated in a flash of wide-eyed, open-mouthed shock. She could feel her knees start to buckle and the edges of her vision start to grey. She was dreaming. This was off the charts impossible. She stumbled back, desperately trying to figure out what had just happened. She wanted to say something but the only sounds that cleared her throat were gasping shrieks of pure terror.

Realizing that maybe he had hit her too soon with too much information, he took the necklace from around his neck, instantly reappearing, which not surprisingly sent her into a full-blown, over-the-top screaming fit. She quickly stumbled backward, catching her heels on the raised brick border along the sidewalk. Moving towards her, he was amazed at how high she went into the air as both her feet went up. The thought of how awkwardly women always fell down flashed through his mind as she thudded to the ground with a groan. Trying to contain his amusement and laughter, he bent down to help her up. "Sweetie, it's okay. Let me help you up. C'mon, give me your hand."

Wide-eyed and with tears of fear running down her face, she stared at him in complete shock. "What, ah, I ah, what did you do?"

He slowly pulled her to her feet and held her close. "It's okay. I just needed you to see what I have been up to today." He chuckled, "c'mon, let's go in the house before the neighbors start coming out."

Once inside, he led her to the living room, feeling increasingly bad about putting her through such a shock. But then again, how else was he going to expose her to the fact that he could disappear and appear at will. It was something out of a movie, something that just could not and did not happen in real life. He knew that he had gone way beyond the borders of normality, and now Sharon knew it too.

"Okay, sorry for the shock, Sharon, but I had to get your attention." He was standing in the middle of his living room more excited than he had ever been in his sixty years on the planet.

Sharon had somewhat collected herself and was sitting on the couch. "All right, how did you do that? And what does it mean?" she questioned sniffing back her tears.

For the next hour and a half he went through every detail of what he had discovered, from hearing about Robashaw's death at the hospital to digging through the contents of the knapsack and finding the medallions and diary.

"So, have you done anything with the second medal?" she asked quietly after he had finished. She had listened to the whole story as calmly as she could, unable to shake the very real feeling that this was a colossal mistake on his part. This was something of great power, and surely other forces of equal power knew about it and wanted it back.

"I don't really know what the second medal does. I have an idea, but I am having a hard time believing it."

"Is that supposed to be funny, Preston? You have a medal that you put around your neck and you disappear. That you believe?"

Confused, he handed her the medal. "You want to try it? It's really cool. I've been doing it all afternoon?"

She recoiled as if the medal were a live snake. "No, I don't want to try it. And I don't want you to do it either for God's sake. This is not a good thing. Can't you see that? It's not normal, Preston. Are you insane?"

He sat down in his easy chair trying to understand why Sharon was having such a negative reaction to what he had discovered. "I thought you would be blown away by this like I was," he replied quietly. "I really thought you would think this was fantastic."

She thought for a moment, trying to put her thoughts into words. "Sweet heart, listen to me. Whatever those things are or whatever they do, including allowing someone to disappear, is not from the natural world, our world, the one you and I live in together."

"So what are you saying?"

"I'm saying that those things cannot be controlled and should not be used. There is no telling what spiritual stuff or dimensional things they disrupt."

"Spiritual stuff?"

"Yes, spiritual stuff, Preston. You think God likes you disappearing on your own like that? Where does that kind of power come from?"

"You're kidding, right?"

"No, I'm not kidding. There is no telling what can happen using that stuff."

"So, why does something like this automatically have to be bad or evil?"

She looked at him as if he had just had a coconut fall out of his ear. "Coins that allow people to disappear are not written about anywhere in the Bible, Preston. I would have seen it."

"So, how do you know Jesus didn't have one of these things around his neck, Sharon, when He did all the stuff He did? You don't know. Besides, you haven't been to church since your dippy sister got married five years ago."

They both sat quietly staring at each other, equally convinced that the other had lost his or her mind.

"So, what are you going to do?" She finally asked, already knowing the answer.

He stuffed the medal in his pocket, taking a deep breath. "I am going to find out everything I can about the medals and Darcy Robashaw. I need more information. Then I will make a decision."

"I'm not sleeping under the same roof as those medals, Preston. I mean it. I don't want them anywhere around me."

"So what do you want me to do? Go to a hotel? Bury them in the back yard? What?"

"I don't care," she announced standing. "I won't stay in the same house with them." She walked out of the room, headed to the kitchen. "I mean it, Preston!" she shouted from the hall. "I want them out."

What was it with wives and this unrealistic fear of anything other than the normal stuff of life? He thought shaking his head. For a second, the thought of putting the medallion back on to give her another chance to really see how cool the whole thing was flashed through his mind. On second thought, the sound of slamming drawers and cussing in the kitchen as she looked for the corkscrew she could never find pretty much let him know that Sharon had had enough *cool* things this evening. *…That could have gone better.*

Chapter Five

July 18th, 2000

Amazing day of discovery. Actually, amazing does not cover it, does not even come close. As I write these words I am overwhelmed with emotion, fear, boundless joy and an excitement I have never felt before. I need to write this down. There needs to be a record of what I am discovering. First of all, I have still not contacted the pastor about all this. Not sure why. And then again, if I were being truthful, I would say that I am afraid that he would tell me to stop messing around with these things and presently that is something I am not prepared to do. So having said all that, I now know what the Gold medallion does...

"Preston, are you down there? I'm getting ready to go. I have to be in Saint Joseph by nine. Preston, can you hear me?"

"Yes, yes, I hear you. I'll be right up. Just putting the final coat on one of the houses. Just a minute," he replied, quickly closing the diary.

They had reached a compromise concerning the medallions. The only way there would be peace in the house is for the medals and all the rest of the things in the knapsack to be kept in the trunk of his car - outside. They were not to be brought in the house, a rule he had already broken when he had gotten up at six this morning, retrieved the medallions and diary, and quietly taken them to the basement.

Sharon was at the sink cleaning up the breakfast dishes when he came up the stairs. "So, tell me you're not going to be running around the neighborhood invisible today," she said looking out the kitchen window, drying her hands. "Tell me you're not going to fool around with those things. I had bad dreams all night."

He walked over and poured himself a cup of coffee. He really did think she was overreacting but kept his opinion to himself. No use stirring the pot anymore than it had been stirred. No matter what he said she was never going to get past her fear of the medallions. Never.

"I promise I will not be walking around the neighborhood even though I still can't believe you don't think this thing is fantastic."

She walked past on her way to the door. "I do think it's fantastic, Preston, fantastically bad. Please don't wait too long before you get rid of it. I'm going to be on edge until it's all gone."

Knowing there was nothing else to say in the argument, he kissed her quickly as she headed for the door. "Call you later," she said, moving off the front porch. Ten minutes after she drove out of the driveway he had the medallions and the diary in hand and was moving into the woods towards Robashaw's camp. There were answers down there, and he intended to find them.

This was the first time he had been in the camp since Robashaw had been carried out. Now, in the daytime, he could see how small Darcy's living area had been. Amazing how different things look in the sunlight. He remembered the campfire being large and bright as he had walked into the small clearing that night. He saw now that the big fire had really been a few small sticks burning in a large coffee can. Robashaw's shelter was nothing more than several long thin tree limbs covered in a blanket and plastic sheeting. Looking around the clearing, he noticed off to his left a mound of dirt similar to the height of a freshly dug grave. Upon closer examination he could see a small pit on the other side of the dirt about a foot deep, three feet wide, and five feet long. The hole had been covered with tree limbs, some old boards, and plastic sheeting. Pulling back the cover, he could see neatly stacked groupings of what looked like bottled water, camping gear, can goods, and clothing. "Cache," he said out loud. Robashaw was building a cache of food and supplies, but why? He sat down on the edge of the hole and started flipping through the pages of the diary looking for any entry that mentioned food or cache supplies. Turning to the front of the book, he found it.

September 18,2000

I have now started the plan. I am getting better at landing and take off. The only injury was last night when I hit the top of the tall cypress as I was trying to land in the front yard. Put some pretty good scratches on my face and hands. Banged up my knee. Dug up my first cache - just basic stuff- up past Haber's ridge. Dug most of the day and got it stocked by six last night. I have marked it on my GPS, - the one David got me for Christmas two years ago. Took me a while to figure out how to use it. I think it will be great. I will list all the cache spots in this journal and also log the locations on the GPS. Anyway, long day yesterday. I am very sore so today is a rest day. As a side note, I woke up this morning and could swear I heard the wife cooking breakfast in the kitchen. Just a dream....,Lord I miss her so....

Preston knew that if he really wanted to get to the facts of how and why Robashaw ended up in Coloma, Michigan, he would have to study the journal from beginning to end. The medallions held power and secrets that needed to be explored. At that moment, sitting in the woods as a cool November breeze rustled through the treetops, he realized that this was something he could devote the rest of his life to. Somehow he would just have to make Sharon understand how important this was. He had closed the book just as the sound of someone moving through the woods caught his attention. There was the sound of voices, laughter, and then the unexpected pungent smell of Marijuana smoke drifting on the wind. They were getting closer. He quickly pulled the silver medallion out of his pocket and draped the chain around his neck. This would be a good test, he thought, watching the now visible teenagers moving in his direction. He recognized the Miller boy, the fifteen–year-old who lived next door, a decent kid who always waved to him on the street. He had never seen the other kid, a tall longhaired type, who even from a distance carried the air of a wise-ass and general malcontent. There is no way Dan Miller would approve of Danny Junior hanging out with this kid, let alone smoking pot.

"Hey, check it out!" shouted the older kid, spotting Robashaw's shelter. He let them walk by within arm's length. He watched as the older kid kicked at one of the support poles holding up the plastic. "You know we should set this shit on fire," he said passing the smoking joint to Danny.

"Why do you want to do that?" he asked, taking the joint. "My house is right over there."

Good for you, thought Preston stepping closer. He was already feeling bad for what he was about to do. But Danny would get over it, and, on the up side, it just might scare the other kid straight, at least for a while. Working hard at controlling his laughter, he stepped up to within inches behind the boys, and in the deepest, raspiest voice he could muster, he quickly whispered, "Never come out here again, or you're dead."

It was as if both boys were suddenly hit with a hundred thousand volts of electricity. The older kid jumped straight in the air, letting out a blood-curdling shriek that sounded like a small animal suddenly being killed. Danny, stunned beyond comprehension, collapsed to the ground into a tight fetal position, screaming uncontrollably.

"Get out of my woods! " shouted Preston, stepping closer to the older kid who was scrambling to his feet in a tangle of plastic sheeting and tree limbs. Danny, several feet away was now on his hands and knees, crawling like some deranged hedgehog through the under brush, leaving one of his tennis shoes behind. The older kid was now in full flight, crashing through the woods as fast as his skinny legs could carry him. Danny had reached the path and was well on his way home, convinced that there were now demons in the woods that wanted to kill him. Neither kid would be back.

Preston took the Medal from around his neck and sat down unable to control his laughter any longer. *God, that was fun,* he thought, wiping the tears from his eyes. *This could be addictive.* Power, that's what he felt sitting there in the woods. For the first time in his life he felt as if he had total control of who and what he was. With this medallion he could do virtually anything. He could take what he wanted. He could even kill with impunity. The thought pulled him up short. *Jesus, where did that idea come from?* That was so far away from his normal nature that the idea would have never normally even surfaced in his mind.

Maybe this is what Sharon was really afraid of. Maybe she had seen what could happen if the emotions that went along with all this were not kept in check. Over the years he had come to rely on her perceptions and insight. Maybe he was blinded by what he had already exposed himself to. Maybe. No, he could keep it together. He was no kid. He would respect the power and do everything he could to keep it in check. If Robashaw had been able to control the medals, he could.

Yeah, he could do this. Just be cool. Study the diary. Follow the lesson that Robashaw had written down and things would work out. Moving through the woods on his way home he let the lies that he just told himself drop to the ground behind him. He had no idea what exposure to this kind of power could do and to be arrogant enough to say otherwise was foolish. No, he now had a firm grip on a whirlwind and there was no telling where he would end up. Terrible, wonderful, and strange things were about to happen and he would be a witness to the drama. Things were just getting started.

Chapter Six

July 28th, 2000

I have discovered something incredible about the second Medallion that I can hardly believe. There are birds in flight inscribed on both sides of the medal. That led me to believe that whoever has this medallion around the neck can fly. This morning I put the Gold medal around my neck and immediately felt it press itself onto my chest, a strange feeling but not at all uncomfortable. I had no idea what to do next so I started walking down my driveway towards Tomlinson road. After awhile I felt the need to run, something I have not felt compelled to do in over twenty years, to say the least. Feeling a bit foolish, I began to trot, hoping none of my neighbors would drive by and catch this sixty-year-old man with bad knees trying to run.

Picking up speed and feeling quite proud of myself, I got a little cocky and increased my stride. That is when I stumbled. This is where it gets crazy. I fell forward, arms outstretched. But instead of falling on my face, I stayed horizontal, four feet off the ground, cleared the end of the driveway and the road...and the barbwire fence on the other side. I rolled into the tall weeds in Mason's pasture. The cows were very interested. By a conservative estimate, I flew a good fifty yards. My God, what have I discovered?

He closed the book and stared at the gold medallion on the kitchen table as if it were about to come alive and crawl off. Sharon had gone to work early that morning and had left a note that she wanted him to get hold of the plumber to fix the upstairs leak. At the bottom of the note she wrote in big, underlined letters: GET RID OF THE MEDALS, TODAY!!

Geez, she was really pushing this thing, he thought crumpling the note. He loved her to death, but he had other things on his mind. Plumbing was not one of them. He picked up the diary and stuffed the medals in his pocket. He needed a cup of coffee and a place to think about his next move. He found his truck keys and headed out the door deep in an idea. The McDonalds in town was always busy this time of day with late morning commuters into Saint Jo along with an army of construction and delivery people jamming the drive-through lines, turning a quick cup of coffee into a fifteen minute wait. Determined not to burn any more time than he had to, he pulled his truck into the farthest slot in the lot while thinking about his next move. He had been to this particular McDonalds a million times and had never looked at it in any other way than being a place to get decent coffee or a burger. Now he was looking at all businesses as possible banks, places where he could take what he needed without anyone being the wiser.

Last night just before he went to sleep, the idea had come to him that money was tight so why didn't he use the medals and get what he needed. He had decided that he would not take anything from the mom and pop organizations, only the big franchise places, organizations that could take the kind of hit he was about to inflict. He wouldn't be greedy but take just enough to make things a little more comfortable financially. Now all he had to do was drop the medal around his neck, walk inside, and take what he needed.

Mustering courage, he pulled the silver medal out of his pocket and pulled the chain over his head, instantly feeling the medal press down on his chest. It was almost like the medallion was alive when it came close to his heart. Just before he opened his door, another car pulled up beside his truck. He would wait until they went inside before he opened his door. No reason to freak people out unless he had to.

An older woman stepped out of the car. A younger woman, who looked to be her middle-aged daughter, got out of the passenger side. Much to his aggravation, the woman stepped up to his outside mirror, bent it back, and started checking her makeup. Just to see her reaction, he hit the horn making her jump and squeal in surprise. It was hilarious watching her look into the side window of the truck, the only thing separating their noses - a thin sheet of glass. Just to give her one more shock, he punched the automatic door lock button, which really made her jump. She made a beeline across the parking lot and disappeared inside, having had enough of the empty truck.

As quickly as he could, he opened the truck door and stepped outside. Looking around the lot, he saw that all the other cars were empty; no one had seen his truck door open and close by itself. He walked across the lot and now faced another dilemma. Heavy glass entry doors don't open by themselves. How was he going to open the door without drawing some sort of attention? He would have to wait and then piggyback on someone else going through. He didn't wait long, as two Coloma police officers walked up and opened the doors. He quickly slid in behind them and stood in the middle of the busy eating area. This was amazing, he thought, scanning the room. He was right in the middle of all this activity and no one could see him. Incredible!

Being careful not to touch anybody, he causally made his way up to the side entrance of the register counter and watched. He watched as several young cashiers punched in the orders and opened the registers. There was a good deal of space between the register counter and the counter filled with all the coffee and ice cream machines, enough room for him to carefully walk up behind one of the cashiers taking orders. As the drawer slid opened, he timed his withdrawal just after she had put bills into the drawer and just before the drawer closed.

Reaching in, he deftly snatched four twenty-dollar bills from the tray. Not knowing what to do next, he stepped back from the register and waited for some kind of response. Nothing. Business went on as usual. Nothing had been seen or heard. Not wanting to push his luck, he carefully walked out of the counter area and headed for the door. He had to wait a good five minutes before another person walked up from the outside and let him out.

Smiling as if he had just stolen the crown jewels, he walked across the parking lot amazed at how easy that bit of larceny had been. Not wanting to cause a stir, he moved to the front of his truck and knelt down. There he removed the Medallion and stood up. The drive-through lanes were now empty, giving him a chance to give back a little of the eighty dollars he had just withdrawn. He liked that word – withdrawn. It didn't bother his conscience nearly as much as saying what it really was - stealing.

As he drove out of the lot, he knew he was going to need some space and time away from prying eyes to begin to test the gold medallion's supposed power. He was still trying to get his head around what the silver medal could do. He could barely imagine how it would be if the gold's power was real. Heading out onto Blue-Star Highway, he remembered a large open field about three miles down that could be just the secluded space he would need. The field was ringed with tall pine trees that shielded its view from the road.

Minutes later he spotted the unmarked dirt road that ran towards the back of the unfenced property. He drove in slowly, parked, and then sat quietly surveying the field. It was still relatively early. Kids were in school, no hunters or woodcutters were around nor anybody else driving tractors or farm machinery. He had the place to himself. Stepping out of his truck, he picked up the diary and turned to the entry about how Robashaw first discovered the power to fly.

Feeling a bit foolish, I began to trot, hoping none of my neighbors would drive by and catch this sixty-year-old man with bad knees trying to run. Picking up speed and feeling quite proud of myself, I got a little cocky and increased my stride. That is when I stumbled. This is where it gets crazy. I fell forward, arms outstretched. But instead of falling on my face, I stayed horizontal, four feet off the ground, cleared the end of the driveway and the road...and the barbwire fence on the other side. I rolled into the tall weeds in Mason's pasture. The cows were very interested. By a conservative estimate, I flew a good fifty yards. My God, what have I discovered?

Okay, he thought putting on both medals. This is where it gets interesting.

The early afternoon sun was just beginning to seep through the cloud cover as he made his way into the field. The ground was surprisingly hard even though the weeds were nearly up to his knees. Looking to his left, he estimated the tree line to be a good two hundred yards away, probably the greatest amount of unrestricted space in the area. He would head in that direction.

Pulling off his coat, he took a deep breath and started a slow trot through the weeds, gradually picking up speed as he warmed up. He hadn't run like this in years. *God, I feel ridiculous*, he thought now running as fast as he could. "Okay, here we go!" he shouted just before throwing his arms forward and leaping flat out like he had seen in the old superman movies. He sailed through the air a solid six feet before crashing into the hard ground with a thud and a groan. He lay face down, smelling the dirt and the tall grass, trying to get back the breath that had been knocked out by the fall. "Jesus," he moaned. *Nothing like having a cell phone and a wad of keys in your front pocket when you slam into the ground.* Rolling onto his back, he looked up into the cloudless November sky. It didn't work, he thought. Robashaw was full of shit.

Embarrassed by his foolishness, he slowly got to his feet and brushed off bits of weed and dirt. *Something wasn't right. The silver medal worked fine. So why didn't the gold?* Confused, he walked back to his truck and laid the open diary on the hood. Maybe he had read it wrong? He checked the entry again.

This morning I put the Gold medal around my neck and immediately felt it press itself onto my chest, a strange feeling but not at all uncomfortable. I had no idea what to do next so I started walking down my driveway towards Tomlinson road. After a while I felt the need to run, something I have not felt compelled to do in over twenty years to say the least. Feeling a bit foolish I began to trot, hoping none of my neighbors would drive by and catch this sixty-year-old man with bad knees trying to run.

"Put the Gold medal around my neck and immediately felt it press itself onto my chest," he read out loud twice. He looked down at the medals and saw that they were hanging free. *Could that be it? He didn't say anything about wearing both medals.* He took the silver medal off and immediately felt the Gold medal press itself against his chest. A shiver of raw excitement ran down his back as he laid the silver medal on the hood of the truck. Holy shit, he thought. This felt different. As he walked further into the field, his mind raced with the possibilities. Could that be it? Could you only use one medal at a time? Could it be that simple? He took a deep breath, looked around, and started a slow trot. Then he started picking up his knees into as much of a sprint as he could muster. "OKAY!" he shouted running full out. "Let's go!" With a grunt, he leaped into his best Superman form and, to his stunned and utter surprise, stayed flat, four feet off the ground as if he had landed on a table. He looked at the grass whizzing by with a hiss below. "Oh, God! Oh, God! " he shouted as he picked up speed. He was really doing it. He was flying. Looking up, he now saw that he was closing fast on the tree line, the pines getting bigger by the second. The wind was now rushing by his ears and pulling tears from his eyes as if his head was outside a car window going sixty miles an hour. "Oh shit!" he shouted, realizing that he was about to kill himself. Just before crashing headlong into the thick stand of trees, he instinctively pulled his arms to his side, arched his back and sat up, preparing to hit the trees feet first. Immediately, to his stunned surprise, he stopped and slowly settled to the ground.

"Airbrake!" he shouted. Sitting up stops forward momentum. Unbelievable. As he lay in the grass, tears rolling down his face from laughing, he realized that he had never felt better in his whole life than at this moment. Never had he felt such absolute, unrestricted joy. *I can fly*, he thought. *Son of a bitch, I can fly.*

Chuckling to himself and still not really believing what he had just done, he stood up and brushed the grass from his hair and shirt. This time he would count the steps it took to get airborne. In his mind, the shorter the distance, the better. Taking a deep breath, he took off running and in five steps leaped forward. Again, he stayed four feet off the ground, the weeds flashing by like a deep brown carpet below him. Seeing his truck coming up fast, he quickly arched his back, sat up, and stopped, again gently settling to the ground. This was mind-blowing, way beyond any outside sensory experience he could think of. Nothing touched this, nothing.

For the rest of the morning he flew short distances and then longer stretches as his confidence increased. He soon discovered that his hand movements controlled altitude: palms flat - he stayed level, palm's up - he gained altitude. He was careful not to go higher than the treetops, trying to limit visibility as much as possible. Palms down - he dropped. In fact, several times he swooped so low that he looked like a plow going through the tall weeds. He discovered that his legs determined forward speed. Knees straight out -maximum speed, knees bent ninety degrees - almost stopped. These were all body movements strikingly similar to skydiving maneuvers. He was surprised at how natural it all felt after only a few hours of effort.

After several hours of testing his newfound abilities, he began to recognize that flying was extremely taxing on his body. His shirt was soaked through with sweat even though the outside temperature was in the low sixties. His body was exhausted and sore from the abuse as he had thudded into the ground several times at a fairly high speed when he became aware of how sensitive the stability of the flight was to cross winds and gusts. Even though he was more tired than he had been in years, he was filled with incredible excitement and a nearly overpowering desire to literally take off and explore the world.

There was a drive to leave everything he knew and had worked for all these years - house, truck, possessions, everything. In that instant he knew what had motivated Robashaw to start living the way he did because he was now infected with the same motivation. There was no turning back now, no more second guessing the right or the wrong of keeping and using the medallions. As he slowly drove out of the field and turned onto the highway, he tried to think of some valid argument for Sharon's outright refusal to have anything to do with the medals. He would not be able to keep the fact that he could now fly hidden. He would have to tell her, and she would just have to understand. She just had to.

Chapter Seven

It was all she could do to keep from turning around, driving down to the new Watervliet Marriott, and staying there until she was sure Preston had taken the medals out of the house. Even though the medallions had been outside in the truck, she hadn't been able to sleep. She knew she would not rest until they were off the property completely. She pulled into the driveway, parked the car, and sat in the quiet, working on her resolve.

She had always prided herself on her ability to keep an open mind, her willingness to try new things. But for some reason, the medallions scared her, brought up a primal fear colored with religious overtones. She could not shake the feeling that the medals had a deeply corrupting power, a force that could change a person in a bad way - forever.

As she walked into the house, Preston greeted her from his easy chair. The ice packs that he held to both of his knees overshadowed the big grin on his face. "Hi, Sweetie."

"What happened? What's wrong with your legs?" she asked setting her purse and shoulder bag on the couch.

"Oh, I'm fine. Just a little sore, that's all."

She sat down on the couch, trying to ignore the lie. She could always tell when he wasn't telling the truth. The way he pursed his lips and smiled without showing his teeth was a dead give-away every time. "What's going on, Preston? I can always tell when you're lying. You're not good at it."

"Jesus, Sharon, you've been home only minutes and already you're giving me a hard time? What the hell?"

"Did you get rid of the medals?"

"What?" he asked, stalling.

"I said..did you get rid of the medals?"

"Well, not exactly. You see, there is something I want to talk to you about."

"That's what I thought," she replied, throwing up her hands in disgust. "I have been begging you to get rid of that stuff, Preston, and you think this is some kind of joke. I'm serious. I want that stuff gone."

"Sweetie, look I…."

"No, no more arguments about keeping the medals or any of that stuff. It's not good, Preston. It's not right and you know it."

"If you would let me finish, Sharon, I wanted to tell you what I now know about the medals. It's incredible."

She got up from the couch, quickly gathering her purse and bag. "I don't want to hear it, Preston. I'll be staying in the Marriott in Watervliet. Call me when those things are off the property. I'm done talking." She walked out the front door, slamming it behind her. As she pulled out of the driveway, she looked back at the house, desperately hoping that he would be outside waving her down. After several moments she slowly drove down the street, not even bothering to look in her rearview mirror. Evidently he had made his choice.

****

August 5th 2000

Today was the first time I was able to gain some real altitude using the gold medal. I was able to pace some cars above Lost Trail Pass. Assuming they were averaging around seventy miles an hour, I figure my top speed is probably around a hundred miles an hour. The problem I am now having is the cold in flight. I am going to have to figure out a way to stay warm. I am going down to the Sporting Goods store in Hamilton today to pick up some goggles, gloves, knees pads, and maybe some long johns.

Trying to figure out what he was going to do about Sharon, Preston closed the diary He had been married to her long enough to know that whenever she was really upset about something it was best to give her some space and just let the steam vent. He still had no idea how he was going to convince her to let him keep the medals without getting a divorce. He was not going to let this go, not after experiencing a taste of power and control far beyond anything he had ever encountered. Sitting in his chair in the living room, he realized that he could literally go or do anything he wanted. There were no boundaries past his own physical abilities. It was something he simply could not walk away from.

Suddenly an idea came to him, and he headed upstairs where he stored his motorcycle racing leathers. Finding them in the back of the closet, he took them off the rack and pulled on the tight fitting jacket. They still fit he thought, pulling on the leather pants. He walked over and stood in front of the mirror, remembering when he first ordered the leathers. He loved the old-school Yamaha logo and the black and yellow colors. They were a bit snug, but they would work to keep him warm in flight. He stepped back in the closet and pulled his full-face helmet off the shelf. Looking in the mirror, he smiled. This would be his flying outfit. This would work. He couldn't wait to start working on getting higher and faster.

The problem he now faced was how to work on it without being seen in the daylight. He realized he would have to fly at night. But then there was the problem with navigation. How would he find his house in the dark from altitude? Another idea flashed through his mind. *How do people navigate at night? GPS!* He took the helmet off and tossed it on the bed before heading downstairs. *That's why there was a GPS in Robashaw's knapsack. The son of a bitch was flying by GPS.* He found the small machine and turned it on, only to discover that the batteries were long since dead. He was pleasantly surprised to see that Robashaw had attached an elastic wristband to the device. The guy had thought of everything. He replaced the batteries and a brightly colored display screen came on. He stood in the kitchen dressed in his leathers adjusting the device on his wrist while working hard to control the building excitement. He had everything he needed. Now all he had to do was practice.

Hearing the front door open, he turned, surprised to see Sharon walking in. She stood in the doorway, confusion and fear etched deep in her face. "What are you doing?" she asked not moving.

Feeling somewhat foolish standing in front of her wearing his full racing leathers, he set the wrist mounted GPS on the kitchen table. "Well, ah, it's kind of complicated. Sweetheart, just hear me out, just for a minute. Just let me explain what I've discovered."

Unexpectedly she walked over without saying a word and hugged him close. "This scares me so much," she said holding him tight. "Tell me it's going to be okay."

He held her at arm's length. "Listen, Baby, I want you to know..I, ah, need you to understand that next to finding you this is the greatest thing that has ever happened to me. It is going to be okay. This is something great! It really is. Please don't be scared." He guided her to one of the kitchen table chairs. "Okay, sit down and let me tell you what I have done."

She slowly sat down with a sigh, not even trying to hide the fear. "Go ahead; I'm listening."

Working hard to keep his exuberance in check, he told her about the diary and the things he had discovered in the journal, how Robashaw was slowly able to work out how the medallions worked. He then went into great detail about his afternoon and how he had learned to fly using things he had read about.

For several moments, she sat quietly. "Preston, answer me this. How will this help us? What do we gain by knowing this?"

"That's an odd question. I'm not sure what you mean?"

"I guess I'm asking - what do you hope to achieve by doing this? Where's it going to lead?"

He sat down in one of the chairs. "Well, I really haven't thought about what I'm *gaining* from having the medals, other than experiencing things and feeling things that I have never emotionally felt before."

"Do you know what would happen to you, to us, if anybody found out you could be invisible or fly whenever you wanted? I mean it's just off the charts."

Preston thought for a moment. "They would probably have me locked up, I guess. I would probably be considered a national security risk."

Sharon nodded solemnly. "Exactly, Preston. There's no way the Government would allow you to do these things. Never."

"Probably right," he replied, sitting back in his chair. "Never really thought about the possible government implications of this. To be perfectly honest, I am just really enjoying myself."

"So what are your plans? Is this your life now? Is this what you're going to do?"

He tried to think of a way to express himself without hurting her feelings. "Sharon, listen to me. You and I both know that I cannot just throw this stuff away. The find is too incredible to do that. As far as what I am gaining? I'm not sure. Maybe nothing. But what I do know is that being able to do these things is power, and I know I can control it. Just give me a chance to find out more about it. Please."

She thought for a moment while staring at her hands. "All right. Do what you need to do. But I want you to know that I am dead set against all of this."

In his mind he knew this would probably be about as much of a concession as he was going to get. "Thank you, Sweetie. I'll be careful."

She leaned over, kissed him, and then left the table.

"So you're not staying at the Marriott?" he asked smiling.

"Don't push it, Preston!" she shouted from the hallway. He knew she wasn't going to leave.

Chapter Eight

When you come out of the tiny settlement of Sula, you turn left up Highway-93 to get to Hamilton, Montana. It is a winding two-lane fare that follows the Bitterroot River, a Mecca for the out-of-state trout fishermen and flatland tourists from all over the country. It was before nine in the morning, the traffic flow was still light, a little early for the logging trucks and about a half hour past the time when the few commuters that still lived in this high country went to work. He liked the drive from his house up on Jenning's Creek to town. Gave him time to think and look at the fantastic scenery. He had been here his whole life but never got tired of looking at the Saw Tooths to the west and the river to the east. He could not imagine living anywhere else. The leaves were just starting to turn. The oranges, reds, and yellows dotting the hillside announced the end of something and the beginning of the heavy whiteness that was only weeks away - maybe even sooner. Winter, a season well respected by the locals, hit hard and fast in this part of the Bitterroot. That respect had heightened his concerns even more for his father's welfare. It had been two weeks since he had heard from the old man. Two weeks without a word was not entirely out of character, but it was long enough to make him and his brother concerned.

The old man liked his privacy, something the boys respected, but he was getting up into his eighties and at that age it was good to keep a close eye, even if the old man didn't like it. The Robashaw's had lived in the Bitterroot Valley since 1874, in Hamilton since the early 1900's. The family had lived, died, prospered and worked in the area ever since Gustavo Robashaw bought a one-way ticket from Alcott, Germany back in 1873. A carpenter by trade, he had headed west to make his fortune. A hundred and ten years later, the Robashaw Construction Company employed eighty people and had built three quarters of the houses and commercial buildings throughout the Bitterroot Valley. Representing the third generation of Robashaws, Carl and his younger brother Frazier now ran the company.

Carl drove his pickup into the BP gas station parking lot just outside of Darby. It was the one station his dad would use to fill up, saying that all the other stations had bad gas, the kind that made a truck run rough. If truth were told, the old man just liked the people who worked the counter, and he would use any excuse to stop by and have a cup of coffee.

"Morning, folks," announced Carl, shaking off the early morning chill as he stepped into the store.

"Morning, Carl," replied the older redheaded woman working the counter. Alice Bauer was a Bitterroot native and a fixture in the area. Her husband of forty years had died of cancer last spring, a loss felt by the entire community. Alice didn't need the work, she had just found it hard to stay in the big empty house alone.

"Alice, have you seen my dad? It's been a week or so since I've seen him."

Alice thought for a moment as she continued to wipe down the counter with glass cleaner. "You know, now that I think of it, it's been awhile since he's been in. Is everything okay?"

Carl poured a cup of coffee from one of the silver pots on the warmer. "Yeah, I think so. You know dad. He goes hunting without telling anyone. Went up to State Line to the casino two months ago and didn't say a word. Been doing that a lot lately."

Alice laughed. "He's a pistol. I'll give you that. If he does drop by, I'll tell him you're looking for him."

Carl tossed a dollar bill on the counter. "I'm going to head over to his house and see if his truck is there."

She smiled, picking up the bill. "If you find that old rascal, you tell him to come by. I miss talking to him."

He pushed his way out the door. "You bet, Alice. I'll catch you later."

As he pulled back onto the highway, a growing sense of unease rolled in his gut. The Robashaws, well known in the community through Masons, Kiwanis, and a dozen other charity and community project groups, were known to have money. He remembered warning his dad several times to not carry large sums of cash with him. The old man was too trusting and thought every person in the valley was a friend. Carl's biggest fear was that someone had followed the old man home and robbed him. Everybody knew the older Robashaw lived alone. He would be an easy target.

Ten minutes later Carl drove up into the large circular drive his father had put in last summer. An odd chill ran down his back as he spotted his father's new Ford pick-up sitting in the driveway next to the front door. "Hey, Dad! You around?" he shouted, stepping from his own truck. Silence. He walked up to the side door of the house, the one that led directly into the kitchen and the only door the old man ever used. "Hey, Dad, you here?" he announced, knocking loudly.

The place was quiet. He tried the handle and found that it was unlocked. "Hey, Dad. It's me, Carl. Are you home?" Stepping into the kitchen, he saw the answering machine blinking the number 8 on the immaculately clean and orderly kitchen counter. It looked as if no one had been there for weeks. He pushed the phone's playback button, discovering the multiple calls he and his brother had left asking how he was and to please call them back.

He searched the rest of the house, his concern growing by the minute. Having checked the house, the small shop out back, and the rest of the property, he knew he would have to do something he had never done before. It was time to call the police.

****

August 28th, 2000

Took my first extended flight last night. Cold as hell. Found out that I can only maintain top speed for about ten minutes and then I get tired. The wind pushing against my neck starts to hurt, and then I am not stable. I can now turn and am working on not losing altitude when I do. Flew from the back yard up to Stevensville. Still hard to judge, but I estimated my height at around 800 feet the entire way. I don't think anyone spotted me. It was very late in the day, around 5:30. Picked up a lightweight helmet and some ski goggles. They help with the wind greatly.

Really tired now. Have to get dinner and go to bed. Still not sure where all this is headed. Don't know who to tell.

Preston closed the diary, comparing his feelings about the medallions to Robashaw's. He still had no idea what this new power could be used for besides ripping off commercial businesses and flying just for the sake of doing it. Sharon had asked the right question: what did he hope to gain out of all this? He knew he needed to know more about what the medals were and why they carried this special power. He felt a need to learn more about Robashaw and how he had ended up in Coloma. Somebody had to know the man. Someone had to be looking for him. Preston had been up all night, unable to sleep. So at 6:30 in the morning, he quit trying and headed downstairs for coffee.

Sharon was in her room, her rhythmic deep breathing indicating a sound sleep. He poured coffee and turned on his laptop, determined to find any information he could about the medallions. One of Robashaw's entries had referred to something called *Heptameron magic.* He scanned the Internet for several minutes seeing a consistent reference to a Dr. Peter of Abano and Heptameron Magic, in particular a magic circle on paper that he had devised in 1310.

Dr. De Abano, also known as Pietro d'Abano, was borne in Italy in 1257. According to the report, he was considered a philosopher and magician, evidently one of great skill, so good in fact, that it led to his imprisonment for heresy where he died in 1315. According to several of his written texts and notes, he was deeply involved with the complex study of metallurgy and in particularly in the properties of silver and gold. Just prior to his arrest, it was said that he had been able to infuse *magical* properties into metal allowing him to do extraordinary things. Through this power, it was claimed that he could *"Retrieve money he had already spent out of thin air."* *(Elucidarium Necromanticum Petri de Abano;* the official transcript of the Inquisition.)

According to a witness at his trial, De Abano was able to be in two places at the same time. After his suspicious death in prison, where he had awaited a second trial for heresy, he was so feared by the church that his body was ordered exhumed and burnt. His remains were removed by friends prior to the burning and were never found even after an exhaustive search by the Inquisition investigators. The good doctor had escaped, even after death.

Preston now realized that there was a very deep and probably a very dark story behind the medallions and their powers. He had been fooling around with something that had the potential to affect him in a really bad way and, if he wasn't careful, could even kill him. Searching the Net, he could only find a limited amount of information concerning De Abano's work, in particular, with coins or metal. He knew if he wanted more, he would have to find translations of some of the books that had been written in his name.

He was most interested in a book consistently mentioned - *Conciliationes Physiognomica* - an ancient tome written by the doctor himself. Believe it or not, it was currently available on Amazon books. Amazing.

Chapter Nine

"Carl, I have the description of your dad but I need a little more information. Have a seat." The Ravalli County Deputy pulled a chair up behind his desk while taking out several report forms. "So tell me a little about your father. I know you folks own the Robashaw Construction Company."

"Yeah, my brother Frazier and I took over running the company in 2000, a year after mom died."

"So your dad lives alone?" questioned the Deputy, writing.

"Yep. Also, you need to know that my father is an intensely private man, always has been, something that has gotten more pronounced since 2000."

"How so?"

"Kind of hard to explain. But we believe he's been taking private chartered flights all over the country for the last ten years."

The Deputy looked up from his paperwork. "Nothing illegal about that, Carl. People can travel all they want."

"That's true. But we've never been able to figure out how he's doing it. We've contacted every charter service in Montana, Idaho, Washington, and California, and none of them had a record of him flying anywhere, ever."

The Deputy leaned back in his chair, "Is your dad a pilot?"

"Nope."

"How about the train? You can catch it in Missoula. Goes all over the country."

"Nope. Checked that too. No passenger tickets have ever been bought from Amtrak."

"Sooo, how do you think he's getting around? Maybe he's driving the hell out of his pickup?"

"Nope. Checked that too. He's had the truck almost a year now and there are still less then thirty-two hundred miles on the odometer. Like I said, we can't figure out how he's doing it."

The Deputy smiled. "Maybe he's doing it now. Maybe he isn't missing. Maybe he just hasn't decided to come home yet."

Carl thought for a moment. "Not this time. Something isn't right. I can't put my finger on it, but I believe there's some kind of trouble."

The Deputy nodded, taking more notes. "All right, let me go over this description again. Let me know if you want anything added. *Darcy Robashaw, DOB 7/14/1938, 5'9, 150 pounds, white hair, blue eyes.* Is that an accurate description of your dad?"

"Yep, that's him. What now?"

"I will put out a BOLO and then add his name and description to the missing persons registry and it will go nation-wide. Then we just wait and see what turns up. If he does come back home, be sure and let me know."

As Carl drove out of the sheriff's department parking lot, he could not shake the feeling that something bad had happened to his father. He had nothing to base the feeling on other than the fact he was gone and had been out of contact for at least a week. As he drove north on 93 headed back up to his father's house, he brushed back a tear. No, this was different. The old man was in trouble. Something had happened. He could sense that life was about to change.

****

Later that same day and eleven-hundred miles away, Preston walked through the front doors of Lake Michigan College, a small junior college with a big academic reputation in Southwestern Michigan. He lived fifteen miles from the campus and had decided to get an expert's opinion concerning the Medallions. Calling the administration office, he had discovered that there were several Art History professors on staff and was told that one of them might be able to give him more information about the medals. It was a shot in the dark but one he felt he needed to take.

After waiting a half hour in the Administration lounge, Preston was finally met by a small, older woman with disheveled gray-black hair who introduced herself as Professor Helen Gilson. Thin and frail, she epitomized the elderly college academic in Preston's mind. She moved with a deliberate gait and surprising speed considering her aged appearance. They walked to a small cluttered office where books and papers were stacked high on the desk and floor. "So, you brought something for me to see," she announced, closing the office door. She slowly sat down at her desk without offering him a chair. In fact, there were no other chairs in the room.

"Ah, yes, here we go," he replied, pulling the medals out of the purple Royal Crown Whisky bag.

The woman gently took the Medallions and laid them on the desk. "And you got these where?" she asked putting on glasses that hung from a gold chain around her neck.

"I picked them up at a yard sale in Grand Rapids a couple of weeks ago." He had been practicing the lie all morning.

She picked up the gold medal and looked through the bottom of her glasses. "Oh my," she whispered, examining the Medallion. For several minutes she turned the coin over and over, looking at every detail. It was as if Preston did not exist, her attention now totally absorbed by the medals.

After several awkward minutes of silence, Preston cleared his throat. "Ah, what do you think?"

She slowly removed her glasses while setting the medal back on the desk. "Mister Dale, you say you found these in a yard sale in Grand Rapids?"

"Yes, Ma'am. I paid ten bucks for the both of them." Again, another practiced lie. "Do you know what they are?"

"Well, I have been studying art antiquities for over thirty years, and in all that time, I have only seen one of these items and that was in the Metropolitan Museum in New York back in the eighties."

"So these things are old?" he asked, starting to feel uncomfortable. He could already tell that she was not buying the lie about the yard sale.

She picked up the gold Medallion. "Mister Dale…"

"Call me Preston, Ma'am. That's my first name," he announced, trying to lighten the mood.

She smiled faintly. "Okay, Preston. These medallions are ancient Kabala healing coins. It's my guess that they could be from the twelfth century...maybe older."

"You can tell all that just by looking at them? Really?"

"It's my opinion. Of course, if you want to show them to someone else, you can take them up to the Antiquities Studies Lab at Norte Dame. Professor Iverson is in charge of the department. I can call him if you would like."

Preston thought for a moment. He really didn't want anyone else to know about the Medallions, much less a professor at a major university. "You know, thank you, but I think I know where to start. I'm going to do my own research for a little bit. Do you think these things have a value?"

She looked at him as if he had just caught fire. "They are priceless, Mister Dale, priceless. Do you intend to sell them? Because, if you do, I know of probably five or six major museums here in the States that would be interested."

Not wanting to prolong the conversation any longer, he picked up the medals and dropped them in the bag. "No, I'm not going to sell them. I'm going to hang on to them. I really want to thank you for your time, Professor. Thank you so much for the information."

She touched his arm just as he was about to turn away. "Mister Dale, please do not be offended, but I am really having a hard time believing that you found such priceless artifacts at a yard sale. Is that really where you found these items?"

Preston did not know what to say. He was not prepared for someone to actually question where he got the medallions. "Yes, Ma'am, the story is true. Got them out of a yard sale. I guess I just got lucky." What else was he going to say? *Well, the truth is, Professor, I stole them off a dead man?*

She smiled that same faint smile that said everything she was thinking but was way too polite to say. It said, *you're full of shit and I know it.*

He thanked her again and let her lead him out of the office. "Ah, Mister Dale, if you would permit me," she announced, just before he walked away.

"Ma'am?"

"Yes, what I was going to ask is, would you be agreeable to bringing the Medallions back at a later date, so that I could show them to some of my colleagues? I know they would be very impressed."

Jesus, this woman never gave up, he thought. "Well, yes, I guess that would be all right." The second he said it, he knew it would definitely *not* be all right. Why did he agree to that? Shit, that was the dumbest thing he could have done.

The woman stepped closer. "Thank you, Mister Dale. That would be wonderful. Could you write down your phone number? That way I can give you a call, after I talk to my colleagues."

Now things were starting to get complicated. What had started out as a simple fact-finding-foray had a possibility of leading to the entire academic community of Southern Michigan finding out about the medals. He was starting to sweat. "Ah, do you have a pen?"

She reached into her sweater pocket, pulling one out. "I don't have a piece of paper, but I can write it on my hand," she replied, smiling that same - *got you by the balls* grin.

"Ah, okay it's...." He rattled off a group of random numbers, being sure to start the prefix with 269, the area code of this part of Michigan. Giving her a bad number was the only thing he could think to do. He knew the minute he got out of sight she would call just to see if he was lying, which he was. *Goddamn, this had been a dumb idea*, he thought, quickly walking out of the building and into the parking lot. He had brought exposure to something he had never wanted exposed. Finding his truck, he quickly drove out the back gate of the campus not wanting to give the now very suspicious Professor any more visibility. "Way to go, Dale, you dumb shit," he mumbled to himself as he turned onto the freeway. "Way to go."

Chapter Ten

Within the higher orders of academia, the alliances and partnerships of all disciplines worldwide run deep. From Physics to Archaeology, there is constant communication and referral, especially in the fields of study that involve discovery or subject advancement. Many in the field of Historical Archeology belong to fraternal orders, some well known, others more obscure. Because this particular field is not definable by geographical borders, the personal relationships made tend to be strong. Modern communications allow members almost instant contact no matter the country of residence. When something of great importance is discovered, the network lights up and every person with a stake or interest soon becomes aware of the information.

Paul Amoretti had been in his office at the University of Palermo working on a paper about the last dig in the Valley of the Kings for several hours. A multi-national group had been allowed into the area by the government of Egypt after a two-year moratorium. He had been grateful for the experience and the chance to contribute to the dig, but at sixty-three he knew the days of spending months on the hard edges of a major dig were fading fast. He was typing the last paragraph of his report when his cell rang. He immediately recognized the United States number. "Mister Iverson, how are you, my friend?"

"I'm fine, Paul. How have you been? Still working at the most beautiful campus in the world?"

Amoretti leaned back in his chair. He had known Iverson since graduate school when he had been a Notre Dame exchange student a lifetime ago. "Yes, and you need to get out of your stuffy office and come to Palermo. The sunshine would do you some good. You do remember what the sun looks like?"

"You know, my friend, we do have sunshine in Michigan?"

"Ah, I remember. The sun is shining but it is 40 degrees outside…not a pleasant memory. Anyway, I know you did not call to talk about the weather in that cold part of the world. What's going on?"

"Well, I have a bit of news that will probably make you happy and sad, maybe both at the same time. Not sure what your reaction will be, so I will get right to it."

Amoretti lit his pipe, putting the phone on speaker. "Go ahead. I'm all ears."

"Okay, I have a dear friend of mine who teaches at a local junior college in the area, Lake Michigan College in the Saint Joseph, Benton Harbor area of Michigan"

Amoretti blew a perfect smoke ring into the air. "Okay."

"Well, my friend, a visitor dropped by her office at school and asked her to look at something he had bought at a local yard sale."

"A yard sale? Isn't that when you Americans sell all your furniture and clothes on the street?"

Iverson laughed. "Yes, I guess you could say that. Anyway, this guy brings in something for my friend to see and… you will never guess what it was."

"I have no idea," he chuckled. "Americans never cease to surprise me."

"According to Helen, he had two perfectly preserved Kabala Healing Medallions - one gold, one silver."

Amoretti immediately sat up in his chair, the information going through him like an electrical charge. "Excuse me, would you repeat that?"

"Kabala Healing Medallions. Isn't that amazing?!"

Trying to contain his excitement, Amoretti shuffled through the pile on his desk trying to find a working pen. "That's amazing, Ben. Can you give me the name of that college again, where Helen, your friend, works?"

"Sure, Lake Michigan College near Benton Harbor, Michigan. I knew you would be interested in the medals. I know you've been working in Judean/ Christian antiquities for some time now."

"Yes, very interested," Amoretti replied, punching the buttons on a second cell phone. "You said that I would be sad about hearing this news? Why?"

Iverson cleared his throat. "Well, that's the strange part. We know the name of the guy who brought the medals in. But we don't know where he lives or how to get a hold of him. He gave Helen a bad phone number and left."

"Ben, I have a colleague on another line. I have you on speaker. Can I have him listen in?"

"Sure, no problem. As I was saying, we know the man's name, but we don't have an address or a phone number to contact him."

"And, Ben, you are sure your friend Helen knows for certain that they are the Kabala Healing Medallions? One gold, one silver?" He said it loud to be sure the person listening on the other phone heard.

"Yes, she was adamant and quite upset that he gave her a bad number. Helen is in her seventies but still very sharp. I trust her word. Anyway, I thought I would give you a call and let you know that the medals have been seen and that we are trying to figure out a way to get in contact with the guy who has them."

"I can't thank you enough, Ben, for giving me the information. Promise me that you will contact me when you have a solid lead on the Medallions?"

"You can count on it."

Just, for my own curiosity, what was the name of the guy who has the medals?"

"Ah, hang on, I wrote it down here. Okay, here it is. The guy's name is Preston Dale. I would assume he lives somewhere in the area of Saint Joe or Benton Harbor, the southwest part of Michigan."

Amoretti repeated the name while writing. "Like I said, Ben, I cannot thank you enough for the information. We'll keep our fingers crossed that he turns up."

"Okay, Paul. It was great talking to you and my best to your wife. I'll stay in contact with you about this. I know it's important."

"Thank you, Ben. My best to your family. I hope we will talk again soon. Ciao, my friend."

"Good-Bye, Paul. Take care."

Amoretti picked up the other phone. "Did you hear?"

"We will have you on a plane in three hours," replied the voice. "How many do you need to come with you?"

Amoretti thought for a moment. "I'll take Foster and Abel. Have them meet me at the plane."

"I guess I don't have to tell you how important this is, do I?"

"No, you do not. This will be taken care of."

"Please use more caution than we did with Robashaw. You underestimated him, and you know the problems that caused."

"I understand. Mistakes will not be repeated."

"Very well. Keep me apprised on your progress, Professor. The Committee will be very interested in your mission."

"I understand. I won't fail. Not this time."

He ended the call knowing full well that he indeed could not, nor would not, be allowed to fail again. Robashaw had escaped using the medallions. Many times they had come close to catching him and retrieving the medals but had failed. It was amazing that he had been able to elude the Tutore so long.

He locked his desk, turned off his computer and desk light, and headed out of the office confident that this time the Medallions would be found and returned. Walking downstairs he looked at the name he had written down. "Preston Dale," he whispered to himself. "Your life is about to change."

****

Oct 18, 2000

I am now able to control my flights with much greater ease, having learned how to turn and pick my landings. I've been experimenting with flying at night. It's amazing how odd and unrecognizable familiar terrain looks in the dark. All last week I had great difficulty finding the house and had to land quite a distance away and walk home. I've been wearing my long johns and goggles, which are helping with the cold. Still, I can only fly at top speed for short distances. It just plain wears me out, and then I begin to wobble and dip something awful. As a side note I have decided not to talk to the pastor about all this. Really don't know what I would say.

He closed the diary, feeling for the first time, a small, yet growing sense of dread. The day had not gone well at the college. In his sincere effort to find out more about the medals, he had opened himself up to discovery. He had no doubt that the professor would call her friend at Notre Dame and that would start all kinds of official inquires. Thankfully all she had was his name, although if they really wanted to run him down, he was sure they could look him up. He could not think of any laws he had broken other than ripping off McDonald's for eighty bucks, money he intended to replace tomorrow.

He rolled over and turned off the nightstand light, deeply bothered by this latest turn of events. No, he thought listening to the wind blow against the windows, if they really wanted to find him, they would. Then what? He had kept the possessions of a dead man. That alone had to be some kind of crime. Rolling into his blankets, he vowed to be more cautious in the future. He fell asleep without a thought of turning the medals in and walking away. Doing so would have solved most, if not all of his problems, problems that were headed his way as fast as a 747 can fly.

Chapter Eleven

Carl Robashaw had just walked in the door when his cell phone rang. He recognized the Sheriff's Department phone number immediately. "Hello?"

"Yes, Carl, this is Deputy Clark at the Sheriff's Department. You filed a report about your father yesterday."

"Yes. Is there some new information?"

There was a long pause. "Carl, there is no easy way to say this, but we've received a report that your father is deceased."

Carl felt his knees go weak, and he slowly sat down on the bench just inside the front room door. "Deceased? I, I don't understand. Where? What happened?"

"We put out a nation-wide NCIC missing person's BOL on your father. Just about an hour ago, I received an email confirmation of a Darcy Robashaw matching your father's date of birth and physical description, having died on the 18th of this month. That would have been almost two weeks ago."

"Where did this happen?"

"The confirmation came from a small PD in south central Michigan, a place called Coloma. I just got off the phone with the Watch Commander there and he confirmed that a Darcy Robashaw was admitted into the Lakeland Hospital in a town called Watervliet, a town next to Coloma. According to the official record, Mister Robashaw died of a stroke on the morning of the eighteenth. I'm really sorry, Carl."

Carl sat in stunned silence, feeling as if all the air had just been sucked out of the room.

"Carl, are you still there?"

"Yes," he replied brushing back a tear. "I'm here. Just trying to get my head around it. I'll come down to the station and pick up the information if that's all right."

"That's fine, Carl. I'll be here till four. I'll be looking for you. And again, I'm sorry to be giving you this kind of news."

"Thank you, Deputy. I'll be down in a bit." He disconnected the call, his head reeling with questions. *Michigan*, he thought. *What the hell was he doing in Michigan?* They had no relatives there that he knew of, not even an acquaintance from that part of the country. After collecting himself, he dialed his brother and gave him the news. Frazier was deeply shaken but agreed to meet him at the Sheriff's office within the hour. Carl asked his wife to start making flight reservations to Coloma, Michigan just before leaving the house. He would be collecting his father's body and hopefully finding some answers. *Coloma Michigan*, he thought, pulling out onto the highway. *What the hell was going on?*

****

Amoretti dropped his bag into the trunk of the rental car and tossed the keys to Foster, the big German. "You drive. I always get turned around trying to get out of this airport." He had flown into O'Hare dozens of times but had only driven to one of the meetings downtown. That had been enough. Even for the well-seasoned, Midwestern driver, Chicago traffic could be a daunting experience.

To the casual observer, the three neatly dressed men had the look of middle management for any one of the thousand companies calling Chicago home. A closer look would have revealed that two of the younger men carried themselves like seasoned soldiers. The small, yet distinguishable scars on their faces and hands told another story. Both were ex-Legionnaires, having served multiple tours from Iraq to Africa. Both had been recruited by The Committee three years earlier and had absolute, nearly fanatical loyalty to the hierarchy and the cause... true believers who would do anything their superiors asked - without hesitation.

Amoretti tapped out *Coloma, Michigan* on the screen of the rental car GPS. "It's about ninety miles from here," he announced easing back in his seat. "Head that way. We'll find a hotel close by."

The German grunted a response and eased into the outbound airport traffic as he thought about the mission. When The Committee had dispatched him in the past, his approach had always been direct. He found that most people responded better to this as opposed to cryptic small talk and vague objectives. He rarely ever used force except for the incident in Spain in '98 when a man, a dealer in antiquities, actually ran from their first meeting and was hit and killed by a car in downtown Madrid. It had been a messy business, but the artifact had been recovered from his safe and returned.

Preston Dale had been easy to find. Facebook, Twitter, along with the blog that he had been writing were all accessed. The blog contained several newspaper articles that he had written over the years. The writings and musing defined a profile that would be extremely useful. Dale appeared to be a frustrated writer with a very limited bank account and no real prospects for the future. Research showed that his income came from a meager social security check and his wife's job. He had no criminal record and seemed to be a paycheck-to-paycheck kind of citizen like most of the American population. This retrieval should be easy; a million dollars, to someone like Dale, would be too hard to pass up.

****

November 15, 2000

It is now too cold to fly for any significant distance. Winter has hit this part of Montana with a vengeance, covering everything in two feet of snow. I have been driving over to Spokane and using the silver Medallion to do a lot of my shopping. I am drawn to the idea of just walking into a store and taking whatever I want. I really don't need the extra pound of coffee or the couple of pounds of steak or chicken I take. It's the act alone that gives me an incredible feeling of power that I fear is very addictive. I am now able to move around large groups of people without being touched or heard. I went into a fairly crowded jewelry store recently and picked out a watch. I took it out of the display case as quiet as smoke, a Rolex, I believe it is called a Submariner - very handsome. I had never stolen anything in my life, but now I find it almost irresistible to not do it. Though I hate to admit it, I fear the medallions are having a negative effect on my personality... Not sure what to do???

Preston closed the diary and stared at the two Medallions lying on his desk. Robashaw was right when he said the medals had a way of affecting one's personality. He was finding that the more you used the medals - the more you *wanted* to use their power. They were addictive. He could feel a strange sort of pull, for lack of a better term. It wasn't an unpleasant sensation but an awareness that he needed to be doing something else. He had noticed that the feeling was growing, and he was now concerned that this new impulsiveness might just push him out the door to places and into actions that he was not quite prepared for.

By three o'clock that afternoon, bored and irritated that the novel he had been struggling to get down on paper just wasn't happening, he closed his computer and headed upstairs. As he passed the living room window, he could see that the rain had stopped. Muted sunlight was beginning to break through the overcast that had been there all morning. "Time to fly," he whispered out loud.

He quickly grabbed his motorcycle helmet, the medals, and the wrist-mounted GPS and headed out the door with a renewed excitement. He had decided that he was going to stay airborne for the rest of the afternoon, determined to see just how high he could go. As he backed out of the driveway on his way to the field, he hardly noticed the white sedan that turned the corner and began heading his way.

Amoretti had seen the truck pull out of the driveway. As they slowly passed it on the narrow residential street, Amoretti was able to get a good look at the driver. "That's him, Foster. Follow him, but at a distance." He checked the picture he had saved on his handheld. It was from the local paper, introducing Dale as a new reporter. "Yes, that's him. Let's see where he goes."

Twenty minutes later Preston pulled off the highway and onto the muddy dirt-access road that ran along the perimeter of the expansive hidden field. He could barely contain himself as he stepped out of the truck and into the wet, knee-high, weeds. He locked the pickup and stuffed the keys and the silver Medallion in the zippered front pocket of his leather jacket. *Can't be too careful with the medal,* he thought, walking out into the field. After looking around, checking conditions, he draped the gold medal around his neck, feeling the odd, yet comfortable, sensation of it sucking down over his heart. Smiling with anticipation, he pulled on his helmet and tightened the chinstrap. He was ready. "Okay," he whispered, "let's fly."

With a burst of raw energy and four bounding steps, he leapt into the air, executing a perfect takeoff. He laughed out loud as he picked up speed and climbed, using his hands and legs. Seeing the tops of the tall pine trees start to get closer, he made a smooth, wide left-hand turn, still gaining altitude. With the helmet on, the wind was much more pleasant. His eyes weren't tearing and he could hear his own breathing. Now just below the cloud cover, he estimated his height to be about a thousand feet. The sensation was very much like skydiving. He had complete control with any movement he attempted. He made a left turn, right turn, and, just for the hell of it, a smooth barrel roll that made him laugh out loud. "My God!" he shouted, pushing up through the clouds. "This is unbelievable." In a flash, he punched through the cold, wet overcast and suddenly found himself above the grayness in bright blue skies and brilliant sunshine. He had never felt more free or alive in his entire life.

The feeling of total exhilaration was almost more than he could stand as he sailed through the sky. He flew, drinking in every second, every sensation. He could slow down or speed up at will, getting better and more precise with every movement and mile that passed beneath him. It was three hours later when he finally started his descent. The overcast had cleared giving him a clear view of the countryside below. As he glided closer to the ground, the air became warmer. He could now smell the trees and the crops. At ten feet off the ground and just at the tops of a stand of browning corn, he pulled in his knees and gently settled onto the plowed soil.

With total abandon he dropped onto his back and laughed until tears rolled into his ears and the adrenaline stopped pulsing. Looking up into the blue sky, he knew that he was never giving up the medals. They were now part of him and nothing was going to change that - nothing.

Minutes later, he collected himself, dusted off his pants, and started walking out of the cornfield. Finding a dirt road, he took his helmet off, letting the sun warm his neck and back as he walked. He spotted a beat-up pickup truck parked on the edge of the road up ahead, its bed full of irrigation pipes. What made him laugh as he walked by was the license plate motto.

"Life-changing, fields of opportunity." I'll be dammed, he thought, smiling. He had flown to Iowa.

Chapter Twelve

Amoretti had heard that the Medallions carried amazing power, things he could only imagine until now. From just outside the wood line, he had watched as someone actually flew using the power of the medals. After all he had seen in his life serving the VCS, seeing a man leave the ground in unassisted flight was absolutely astonishing. It had been hours since they had watched Dale fly from the field and now the sun was beginning to set, throwing long shadows over the area.

"What do you want to do?" questioned Foster, leaning back in his seat. "I still can't believe what we saw."

Amoretti thought for a moment while lighting a cigarette. "Okay, it's getting dark. We know where he lives. Let's get back to the hotel. We'll come back in the morning."

Driving back to the Fairfield Inn in Watervliet, the men were silent. All three had been shaken by the sight of a man flying, the spectacle reaffirming the enormity and importance of their task. Amoretti opened the file on his lap, trying to see if there was anything he had missed. Over recorded time, the Medallions had played a major part in shaping the social and religious fabric of the world. Originally there were twenty-four medallions - twelve sets. For years, Amoretti had studied the origins of the medallions and who owned them. He had tracked them over the four corners of the world. It was a mission he had gladly accepted.

The Vatican City State, or VCS had established the Congregatio de Auxiliis in 1592 under the direction of Pope Clement the VIII to specifically track down and retrieve the Medallions, fearing their power and influence on the masses if not controlled. The first record of their existence was just after the Apostles met in the upper room as recorded in the book of Acts. It is said that the twelve disciples were given the Medallions as a tool to help them spread the Gospel throughout the world as written by the Sadducee Arontisis in seventy-one AD. For centuries there had been a deep division of opinion within the Ecclesiastical community. Some questioned if the medals were really part of the Gospel lineage. While some spoke of their important place in history, others questioned if they held any real power at all. After what he had witnessed tonight, there was no doubt in his mind.

Amoretti had been a member of The Committee since his graduation from the University of Milan in 1974. He had been recruited directly by the Vatican, who had underwritten most, if not all, of his research over the years as payment for his loyalty and service to the Holy See. He had been a devout Catholic from his youth, never wavering from the faith.

For the last ten years, Amoretti had been one step behind Robashaw, and now his target was in sight. This was the last set of medals that needed to be retrieved. During the end of World War Two, it was believed that the Nazis had stolen this specific set of Medallions from the religious sanctuary in Lyon, a sanctuary for thousands of religious and other priceless artifacts from all over occupied Europe.

The Medallions had disappeared for more than sixty years, gone with the assumption that they would never be found. Then in late 2000, they had surfaced in the United States. A history professor at the University of Montana had seen them when they were brought in by a man named Darcy Robashaw. Mr. Robashaw had won them at a local auction. According to the report, the medals had been part of a local sale, the estate of the surviving wife of a WWII GI by the name of Cecil Tomkins. Tomkins had been a life-long resident of Hamilton, Montana, a hardscrabble cattleman who talked little of his experiences during the war. It wasn't until after his death in 2000 that it came to light that Tomkins had been a highly decorated veteran of the First Infantry Division, Big Red One. He had kept his counsel and pain of the horrors of war for many years.

As they drove into the hotel's parking lot, Amoretti closed the file; the strain of the day had given him a dull ache just behind the eyes and a strong need to sleep. He hadn't felt this much jet lag in years. He would confront Dale in the morning. He would try to get him to see how important it was for him to relinquish the Medallions. A million dollars was a very good incentive, but he knew they would get them regardless. He needed to find out how Dale had acquired the medals in the first place. Where was Robashaw, the old man they had been trying to track down for years? The man's survival had been an anomaly, a mistake that would not be repeated.

In his room later that night just before drifting off to sleep, Amoretti let his mind drift to the memories of encounters with other people who had possessed the things he needed. *Objects* stirred the heart and clouded judgment, a flaw in human nature he had seen countless times. Men of position, intelligence, and influence would hold on to the object, the manuscript, or whatever other *thing* they had acquired till the very last moment. Even when faced with certain death, each still held on to *possession*.

Having seen Dale use the Medallions, he felt affirmed in his opinion that Dale would not give up the medals easily. Unfortunately, he would join the legion of individuals that died or disappeared mysteriously. Death could be the only remedy for the sickness they all shared - the fatal disease of enlightenment.

The revelation of the Gospels and their tenants was far more complex and powerful than the masses knew. The Canons of spiritual law and the Church's written and practiced mandates could not, would not, be threatened. It was a matter of maintaining the social order of the faithful, order that had been protected since the crucifixion of Christ.

He had justified the killings over the years as a just and correct response to an unjust situation. The men and women he had dealt with had no intention, in the beginning, of facilitating their own demise. They had been seekers, brokers, or just normal people who suddenly found themselves in possession of something far beyond their ability to control. This would be the case with Dale. He would have to be dealt with. It was the part of the job that Amoretti liked the least. Within minutes, rationalizations of *murder most perfect* had chased him into his dreams.

****

Seventy miles away and at a steady height of eight hundred feet, Preston struggled to stay on course on his way back to the field where he had parked his truck. His GPS was hard to read in flight, and slight turns threw off the direction indicator. In addition, the sun had just set, making any visual references to the ground hard to read. This was his first real experience flying after dark and it was proving to be far more difficult than he thought it ever would be. He now found that in a low visibility situation he needed to slow his speed. To stay on course, the three-hour balls-to-the-wall flight to Iowa was taking a solid four-and-a-half to five hours back. Sharon would be home from work by now, he thought, and would be climbing the walls wondering where he was.

At last, he could just barely see his white truck in the gloom five hundred feet below and off to his right. The wind had died down but the temperature had dropped, making the last few miles of flight a finger-numbing chore. Clearing the treetops by inches, he pulled his knees up and stopped in midair, slowly settling to the ground. Raising the shield of his helmet, he scanned the darkness looking for anyone who might have seen or heard his arrival. The field was quiet, only the distant sound of geese honking high above.

Getting into his truck, he turned the heat up as high as it would go, trying to thaw the chill that had gone deep. He checked his cell phone as he drove out of the field and discovered that Sharon had called five times. He thumbed the recall button as he pulled onto the highway. "Hi, Sweetie," he announced, hearing her pick up.

"Where are you? I've been calling all afternoon."

"Well, Baby, I went to Iowa. Just landed ten minutes ago. It's been an incredible day."

There was a long pause on the phone. "You went to Iowa? You're kidding, right?"

"Nope, took me three hours to get there and a little over four and a half to get back. It's really hard navigating in the dark; had to go *really* slow."

There was another long pause. "Preston, do you realize how crazy this conversation sounds? I mean really?"

Preston laughed more from relief than anything. "I know, Baby. I can hardly believe it myself. I have to figure out a way to use my cell when I'm in the air."

"Sooo, you're planning on doing this again?"

"Sweetie, listen, I will be home in ten minutes and then we'll talk. This is really something. It really is. I'll be right there."

Pleasantly surprised that she sounded more confused than mad, he switched off the phone. There was no way on earth that he could fully express his feelings about the long flight over the phone. This had to be done face to face.

Four miles away, sleeping soundly in their beds, were the three men who had the ability to change his life forever, guardians of the secret, righteous killers. As if the night were breathing, a cool November breeze rustled through the Coloma woods, a whispered warning.....*Beware.*

Chapter Thirteen

By eight o'clock the next morning, Carl Robashaw had landed in South Bend, picked up his rental car, and was headed to Watervliet to claim his father's body. Frazier, his younger brother, had decided to stay in Montana and run things until Carl could get back. As he drove past the *"Pure Michigan "* state-line sign, he grappled with the surrealness of the day. He was still having a hard time believing that the old man was actually dead. The man who went bear hunting in the Cascades alone last year, the man who cut down half an acre of old growth pine on his property alone last summer …was dead.

The most nagging questions continued to be - how did he get here and why? There were no private flights booked under Darcy Robashaw within the past year. He had checked. No car rental charges, no train tickets bought, nothing. And yet, he had died in a town no one in the family had ever heard of, without answers of how he even got here.

Thinking back over the last several years, Carl had to admit that his father had become even more reclusive than his normal standoffishness. It was a trait every one in the Robashaw family and the Hamilton community had accepted and respected.

It hadn't been uncommon for the elder Robashaw to leave on hunting trips for weeks without telling anyone where he was going or when he would be back. If he did not return the phone calls, all Carl had to do was go to his house and check the gun racks. If the 300 Magnum was gone, the old man was hunting bear somewhere. If the 30.06 was missing, he was looking for antelope or mule deer. Robashaw loved to hunt and did so well past the age when most men stopped heading into the mountains alone.

Carl smiled, remembering how proud his dad would be when he dropped off some of the deer meat he had taken on his hunt. In his normal, soft-spoken way, he would knock on Carl's door, and when he answered, his dad would just point to his truck and say he had some steaks for the kids. It was never hamburger, or roast, or ribs, but "steaks for the kids." It was the old man's way of saying he loved them and that he only wanted the best for his sons and grandkids. Not an overly demonstrative man, that was about all the *warm and fuzzy* you were going to get from Darcy Robashaw.

Following his GPS, Carl found the hospital in Watervliet and pulled into the nearly empty parking lot. He had called the day before and set up an appointment with the physician who had treated his father, a Doctor Nees. After he had inquired at the nurse's station, the doctor was paged and he was directed to Nees's office. The young physician met him at the door of the office, a small cluttered affair that appeared to be nothing more than an oversized closet.

"Mister Robashaw," he announced extending his hand, "please come in. Have a seat."

Carl stepped into the tiny room and pulled up a metal chair. "So you're the doctor who treated my dad?"

The young physician sat down on the other side of the desk while opening a manila file. To Carl, he looked to be about nineteen and carried the air of a young up and comer, someone who had hit all the shiny spots in life and had been blessed with an intellect and good looks that would open all the right doors.

"Yes, I treated your father, a Mister Darcy Robashaw. We were treating him for a broken ankle upon his arrival."

"How did he get here?"

"Excuse me?"

"Do you know how he physically got to the hospital?" asked Carl.

The doctor flipped through his small stack of papers. "Ah, lets see here. Okay, here it is. He was brought in by ambulance and admitted to the emergency room at 2:27 AM on the 18th."

"Does it say where the ambulance picked him up?"

"Ah, nope, there's nothing here in the charts that says where he was picked up. But you know, now that I think of it, your father did say that someone was letting him camp on their property. I'm trying to think of the person's name he mentioned."

Carl thought for a moment, anxious to let the doctor know that his father was not a vagrant. The doctor's tone hit him wrong; it was colored with an unmistakable tinge of judgment.

"You know, Doc, my father wasn't homeless."

Nees sat back in his chair. "Really?"

"My father is the founder and owner of Robashaw Construction in Hamilton, Montana. We have one of the biggest family owned construction companies in the state."

Nees seemed genuinely surprised. "Wow, I had no idea. What was he doing in Michigan?"

"I was going to ask you the same thing. Did he say anything about why he was here or what he was doing?"

The doctor thought for a moment. "No, not that I can remember. I did ask him about all the injuries he had."

"What kind of injuries?"

"I can show you his x-rays. Your father had several healed fractures, some deep bruising, and evidence of soft tissue damage in various stages of healing. They were wounds similar to that received in a car accident. I've never had a patient with your father's advanced age with that much trauma to the body. He really was banged up."

"Jesus," whispered Carl. "What did he die of?"

"Your father died of a stroke, a massive one. It was almost instantaneous. He didn't suffer; I can assure you of that."

Carl took a deep breath, trying to absorb all the odd information Nees was telling him. "Okay, I'm here to claim the body. How do I do that?"

Nees gave him a strange look. "Ah, you weren't told?"

"Told what?"

"Ah, Carl, I hate to break this kind of news but your father's remains were classified as indigent and he was cremated day before yesterday. It had been two weeks since he died, the allotted time for remains reclamation in the State of Michigan. I am sorry."

Carl slowly stood up, seriously thinking about tearing the office apart. "You have got to be shitting me! Cremated? The State cremated my *father*? "

Nees cleared his throat while shuffling his papers. "Yes, I'm afraid that's the case. I really am sorry, Carl."

Carl took several deep breaths, working hard at calming down. "Where are the ashes? Did the *State* get rid of those too?"

Nees checked his file. "No, the remains are being held at the county morgue in Saint Joseph. I'll give you the file number."

****

Less then four miles away, Amoretti, along with his two assistants, pulled their rental car into the driveway of Preston Dale's residence. Foster stepped out of the car and tucked the thin black metal device under his coat. It was his weapon of choice.

The pipe, resembling a ten-speed bicycle pump, was actually an aerosol delivery weapon, capable of delivering a deadly blast of cyanide gas. Once inhaled, the victim dropped almost immediately, leaving only the smell of bitter almonds and a corpse. It was a clean, quiet, and highly effective tool of the trade, a system first used on two Soviet defectors by the KGB in Berlin in 1978. Both men had been found dead behind the wheel of their cars, victims of apparent heart attacks.

Walking up the sidewalk to the front door, Amoretti touched the arm of the big German. "First we talk. Hopefully, we are dealing with a reasonable man. I will tell you when to use that. Are we clear?"

The German nodded and smiled. "Yes, I understand. I am in no hurry."

Chapter Fourteen

It had been a relatively good night. Sharon had been cautiously upbeat about his flight to Iowa, full of questions and wonder about the trip. He wasn't sure if she was buying into the whole idea or just coming to the realization that he was never going to give up the medals willingly and that fighting with him would do little good. They ended up sleeping in the same room, talking late into the night.

He had just poured his coffee when the doorbell rang. He checked his watch. *Nine o'clock on a Sunday morning was an odd time for visitors.* Opening the front door he was greeted by three men he had never seen before. "Mister Dale?" announced one of the men.

Preston nodded. "Yes, what can I do for you?" The man stepped forward, a little too close for Preston's comfort. "Mister Dale, we need to talk to you. My name is Paul Amoretti and these are my associates, Mister Foster and Mister Abel. We are from the Vatican. I'm sure you know why we are here. Can we come in?"

****

Across town, Carl drove out of the hospital parking lot, intent on finding the last person who had talked to his father. The hospital ambulance records said that they had been dispatched to a residence in Coloma owned by someone with the last name of Dale. Following the GPS, he found the house at the end of the block and pulled into the driveway.

*****

Preston had just shown the three men into the living room when the doorbell rang again. His head was already spinning with the idea that three representatives from the Vatican were sitting in his living room, obviously here about the Medallions. *What else could it be?*

Preston quickly opened the door. "Yes, can I help you?"

Sharon, still in her bathrobe, walked up behind him. "Honey, who are the men in our living room?"

"Ah, sorry to bother you, folks, but my name is Carl Robashaw, and I think you called an ambulance for my father two weeks ago?"

Sharon drew a startled gasp. "Sharon," announced Preston, sharply, "go back upstairs. I'll take care of this."

"I'll tell you what, folks," replied Amoretti, suddenly walking up behind Sharon. "Why don't we all come in and sit down. I'd like to speak to Mister Robashaw myself."

"And you are?" questioned Carl, not moving from the porch.

Amoretti smiled. "Someone who may have some answers for you."

On the verge of panic, Preston stood back from the door, motioning for Carl to come inside. Tentatively, Carl stepped in, nodding to Sharon. "Good morning, Ma'am. You have a very nice home."

She pulled her housecoat collar tight. "Thank you. I, ah, I'll be upstairs getting dressed. If you'll excuse me." She gave Preston a quick, worried look and headed upstairs.

Amoretti pointed to the living room. "Shall we?" The three walked into the living room where Foster and the quiet Mister Abel were waiting.

"Okay, Mister Amoretti, what's this all about?" questioned Preston, already knowing the answer.

Amoretti sat down on the couch with a sigh. "Okay, first off, Mister Dale, we know you have the Medallions, the same Medallions that Mister Robashaw had in his possession for several years. "

"Ah, excuse me?" interrupted Carl. "You have something that belonged to my father? What's going on here?"

Amoretti waved his hand, smiling. "Actually they do not belong to your father, Mister Robashaw... Nor to you, Mister Dale. They belong to me, and I would like them back, please."

Carl was getting more confused and angry by the second. "Okay, who the hell are you people and what does all this have to do with my father? No, don't answer that. I think the police will want to know that answer." He started towards the front door.

"I'll tell you what, Mister Robashaw, my associates will follow you to the police department. I think we need to see them also."

Carl stepped out onto the porch on his way to his car. "Suit yourselves!" he shouted.

Amoretti nodded to the big German, who was already moving to the front door with Abel close behind. "Mister Foster, please render as much assistance to Mister Robashaw as you can. I think you have everything you need." The German nodded solemnly and followed Carl outside.

Carl quickly got in behind the wheel of his rental car and started backing out of the driveway. Just as he was putting the car in drive to head down the street, Mister Foster knocked on his window. "Just a moment, Mister Robashaw. Do you know where the police department is? We will follow you."

Carl rolled down his window. "Listen, pard, I don't know you, so just stay the hell away from me. You want to go to the police? That's up to you." Just as Carl was about to roll up the window, he saw the big man point a black metal pipe towards him. "What the hell is tha...? " Fisssht. A sudden moist blast of bitter smelling liquid hit him in the face. In stunned surprise, he rolled up the window as the big man quickly turned and walked away. Instantly, a vice-like pressure hit him in the chest as if he had been shot through the heart. He struggled to drive forward, his feet and legs twitching with uncontrolled spasms. His vision began to blur as a thin, long stream of snow-white mucus dripped from the side of his mouth. His car slowly eased down the street, coming to a stop halfway down the block after rolling into a large pine tree. Carl Robashaw was dead.

"Mister Dale," announced Amoretti walking to the front door. "In several minutes you will see how much we want the Medallions. I suggest that you carefully consider the ramifications of not turning them over to me."

"Are you threatening me?" questioned Preston. "Because if you are, I can always go to the police and tell them what's going on."

Amoretti stopped at the front door. "Well, if you feel you have to do that, be my guest. They will be.." he looked over his shoulder, "just down the block soon. It looks like you won't be bothered by Mister Robashaw anymore. He was the least of your worries." In the distance, a siren could be heard moving in their direction.

Amoretti opened the door to leave. "Ah, here they are now. Well, Mister Dale, I will expect you in the Fairfield Hotel parking lot at nine o'clock, tomorrow morning …with the Medallions. If not..well… I can assure you we will use every bit of our considerable ability to persuade you otherwise. Are we clear, Mister Dale?"

Preston could now see the ambulance and the Coloma Police units pull up next to Robashaw's car. "Jesus Christ," he whispered, stunned. "What happened? Is that Robashaw's car?"

Amoretti stepped out onto the porch. "Mister Robashaw, I'm afraid, has had a fatal heart attack. Very sad." He announced, "Oh, as an added incentive, I will transfer one million dollars into an offshore account in your name, of course, for the return of the Medallions. Conversely, if you decide to make things difficult, please know that we have full access to all of the IRS, DOJ, Homeland Security computer databases. We can turn you into a *very* nasty person with just a few key strokes."

He stepped off the porch smiling. "So, I will expect you at nine o'clock sharp tomorrow? Have a nice day, Mister Dale." He quickly walked across the yard, toward his associates who were already waiting in the car. In total shock, Preston stood in the doorway, watching Amoretti's car slowly pass the frantic activity half a block away, the ambulance and police lights flashing. He slowly closed the door, realizing that in the span of fifteen minutes his life had changed forever. He had no doubt that Amoretti would do exactly what he had said.

"I heard what he said to you," Sharon announced, her voice barely a whisper. She now stood in the middle of the room behind him. "That poor Mister Robashaw. My God, Preston, they killed that man. When is this going to stop?"

"So what do you think I should do?"

She looked at him as if he had suddenly grown a third eye in the middle of his forehead. "You're kidding, right? You're going to give these people the medals. You don't have a choice. They win. You can't fight this."

He walked up and pulled her close. She was trembling, uncontrollably. "It's okay. I'll give them the medals," he whispered. "It's okay."

Outside, the ambulance crews had already loaded Robashaw's body and were driving away. Preston watched through the living room window, struck by the irony of the scene. It was the same ambulance crew that had transported the older Robashaw. He would never be able to explain all of this when the police connected the dots. Two men from the Robashaw family had died and their strange connection to him would soon be discovered. There was no way they wouldn't.

Across town, Amoretti and the other two men slid into the restaurant booth and ordered coffee from the waitress. The place was full of locals, totally oblivious to the men and their business in town. They continued conversations about taxes, school board dramas, about how corrupt all politicians are, the things people talk about in small towns all over the country. Amoretti hit the speed dial on his phone. "Yes, we will have the items in the morning. Thought you would want to know." The waitress walked up with the pot of coffee. Amoretti smiled and waited until she had finished before continuing the conversation. "No, there have been no complications. We are dealing with reasonable people here. Yes, we will be flying out tomorrow. Thank you, sir. I will contact you when we get back to Rome. Good-Bye."

Chapter Fifteen

Later that afternoon, Carl Robabshaw's body was delivered to the Nichols Funeral home in Saint Joseph. The preliminary report from the Medical Examiner as to the cause of death was cardiac arrest. There had been no outward signs of trauma to the body, nor were there any drugs or alcohol found at the scene. Jim Mark, the shift commander at the Coloma PD when the call came in, was responsible for doing the preliminary report on the accident and subsequent death of Carl Robashaw.

He had been going door to door within a block of the accident, looking for anyone who may have seen or heard anything of significance prior to the accident. He pulled into the driveway of the last house on the block and checked the computer to get a name associated with the residence. "Dale, Preston and Sharon," he mumbled, reading the MDT screen out loud. Checking out on the radio, he left his unit and headed for the front door.

Preston was already coming downstairs, having seen the marked Coloma Police unit pull into his driveway. He took several deep breaths, willing himself into calmness. He opened the door on the second knock.

"Morning, Officer. What can I do for you?"

"Ah, good morning, Mister Dale?"

"Yes, that's me. Is something wrong?" The officer smiled. "No, sir. The reason I'm here is that there was a traffic accident just down the street, and it was a fatality."

"A fatality? The speed limit is only ten miles an hour."

"Yes, sir. I'm aware of that. It's just that the guy was not from around here, and I was wondering if you had any contact with him prior to the accident."

Preston thought for a moment. *This was the tipping point in all of this. This is when he would either face the music or try and cover his tracks. The rest of whatever life he had left hung on the answer.* "Ah, no, haven't seen anyone this morning. Just curious, Officer, where was the man from?"

Marks turned to leave. "According to his driver's license – Montana. Sorry to bother you, Mister Dale. I need to get moving. Have a nice day, sir."

Sometimes the consequences of a man's actions are revealed before they even take place. The cosmic law of justice can sometimes correct a great wrong. Emotions are stirred, introspection that would normally take place over a lifetime flashes through the mind in a microsecond - changing everything. Preston felt that cosmic shift as he watched the officer walk away. "Sir," he called stepping out onto his porch, "I need to talk to you."

Marks stopped in the middle of the yard. "Okay, what's up?"

"Ah, you're going to need to come back in."

"Mister Dale, I am really busy right now. Can I drop by later this afternoon? I'm in the middle of this investigation."

"I know the man who died in that car. His name is Carl Robashaw, and he was here asking about his father. His father was Darcy Robashaw, the man who was taken out of the woods behind my house with a broken ankle two and a half weeks ago. "

Marks was quiet for a moment. "Yeah, I think we need to talk," he replied, walking back to the porch.

Preston led the officer into the living room where they both sat down. Sharon quietly walked into the room, her face tight with tension. "Officer, this is my wife, Sharon."

Marks smiled and nodded. "Jim Marks, ma'am. Pleased to meet you." He looked over at Preston. "Why don't you start from the beginning, Mister Dale," he said, taking out a small notebook.

Preston cleared his throat. "Well, it all started when I met Carl Robashaw's dad a couple of weeks ago."

As Sharon sat and listened to Preston relate the events that had led up to today, she felt a growing, powerful sense of relief. She had been living in constant fear the entire time the medals had been in the house - fear of their power, fear of what they were doing to Preston because his behavior had changed, and a deep-seated dread that she would not be able to stop it. She listened as he told Marks that the older Robashaw had entrusted him with his knapsack before he went to the hospital and died, that he went through the bag and found certain *objects* that were better off being shown than talked about.

"If you give me a second," continued Preston, "I'll get the things I found in the bag. "

"Okay," replied Marks, scribbling in his notebook. Preston went upstairs to his bedroom and took the medals out of the Crown Royal bag that he kept on the nightstand by the bed. As he walked back down to the living room, he felt as if a great weight had been lifted off his shoulders. He hadn't felt this good in weeks.

"Officer Marks!" he shouted just before walking into the living room. "I'm going to show you something. Don't be alarmed. Sharon has seen this before."

"Ah, okay," replied Marks warily. "No weapons please."

Preston draped the silver medal around his neck before walking into the room. "I promise," he chuckled. "No weapons." As quietly as he could, he stepped into the living room, watching Marks closely. As he stood less then six feet away from the officer, it suddenly occurred to him that this was the first time he had shown anybody, except for Sharon, the silver medal's capability. He remembered how she had reacted, which had been really funny, but she hadn't been armed. Officer Marks was. *Maybe this was not such a good idea after all.*

"Mister Dale, I really need to keep this moving," he called. "We need to wrap this up."

Taking a deep breath, Preston pulled the Medallion from around his neck and suddenly appeared in the middle of the room.

To Preston, the response to his sudden reappearance, less then three feet away from Officer Marks, went pretty much as expected. For Marks, it was if he had been electrocuted and then hit with a bucket of ice-cold water. Dale had materialized out of thin air, an astonishing thing to see. Marks sat, open mouthed, with his hand on his gun, not sure whether he was supposed to run, laugh, or cry.

"Don't shoot, Officer," laughed Preston, holding up both hands. "I had to show you this so you would believe me. It's beyond incredible."

Marks sat back on the couch and looked over at Sharon. "You just saw him do that, right? I'm not the only one?"

Sharon smiled weakly. "Yep, it's real. We're in real trouble, huh?"

Marks shook his head. "Ah, Ma'am, I *really* have no idea what to say." He looked up at Preston. "Do that again, Mister Dale, but slowly."

Preston draped the chain around his neck and instantly vanished. "Holy shit," whispered Marks.

Preston walked over to his easy chair, sat down, and removed the chain from around his neck." What do you think?" he asked smiling.

Marks stood up, his mind a blur. "Okay, Okay," he replied, starting to pace. "This is beyond my pay grade. Hell, this is above anyone's pay grade." He looked at Preston. "You say you have *two* of these things?"

"Yes, one gold, one silver."

Marks thought for a moment. "I'm almost afraid to ask, but what does the other one do?"

Preston took a deep breath. "The other medal allows a person to fly."

"What?"

Preston smiled, nodding. "Yeah, it gives you the ability to fly. Off the scale amazing, huh?"

Marks slowly sat back down on the couch. "You have got to be shitting me?" He felt as if he was about to pass out. "Fly? As in leave the ground flight?"

"Yep, flew to Iowa yesterday."

Marks let out a high nervous laugh. "You flew, invisible, to Iowa? Yesterday?"

"Well, not exactly," replied Preston. "You cannot use the medals at the same time. What I mean is… they only work one at a time. You're either invisible or you can fly. They seem to cancel each other out if you try and use both."

"We're in real trouble huh?" repeated Sharon.

Chapter Sixteen

By six the next morning, a SWAT unit comprised of members from the Berrien County Sheriff's Department and the Coloma Police Department had set up a perimeter around the Fairfield Inn. Every guest had been evacuated, leaving only room 213, 217, and 219 occupied. Well before the law enforcement started moving into the area, Foster and Abel had arisen. They were now in Amoretti's room, quietly drinking coffee.

Amoretti let out a deep sigh and sat back in the room's large easy chair. "You know, I really thought he would do what we asked." Foster opened the small pillbox and handed them each a small dark capsule. "The price of failure," he announced smiling.

Amoretti hit the speed dial on his cell phone. "Hello, Your Eminence, I just wanted to let you know how deeply sorry we are for failing in our mission. I have texted the location where I believe the items will be stored, at least for a short time." There was a long pause as he listened to instructions from the other end of the line. "Yes, that is being handled as we speak. We gambled this time and we lost."

Abel stood up and walked into the bathroom closing the door behind him. Foster took off his shoes and lay back on the bed. Amoretti smiled at the big German. "Good-bye, my friend. I will see you in paradise."

Foster smiled back, winked, and then bit down on the capsule. He was dead in seconds. Amoretti reached over and parted the curtains slightly to get one last look at the deep purple sky of a pending sunrise. From his second floor window he could see at least ten police cars below. "Good-bye, gentleman," he mumbled, biting down on the capsule. His body stiffened, then spasmed with one last jerk. He never heard the room's door smash open, nor the flash bang that detonated just under his easy chair. Death had taken him instantly.

Getting the all clear, Marks, along with three other detectives from the Berrien County Sherriff's Department, walked into the still smoke-filled hotel room. The Def Tec flash bang had blown out the room windows, leaving the thin white curtains gently blowing in and out of the hole like a flag.

"Jesus," whispered Marks, checking the pulse of the man reclining in the easy chair. "There's not a mark on this guy."

"The same goes for this one," announced the Sheriff's detective as he checked the man on the bed. He bent down close to the German's face. "Smells like bitter almonds. The skin is an odd red color." He looked over at Marks. "I'm thinking poison, maybe cyanide."

"Hey guys," announced one of the uniformed deputies, stepping out of the bathroom. "There's another one in here."

Marks stepped into the large bathroom and checked the pulse of the man crumpled in the tub. He was fully clothed and carried the same strange smell of bitter almonds. All three men had killed themselves with cyanide. Daryl Grey, the Coloma PD Chief, walked into the room. "Hey, Marks, you want to step out here for a minute? I need to talk to you."

Marks nodded. "Sure, Chief. Hey, guys, go ahead and start the log. Nobody in or out except the ME and the Departments CIs."

"No sweat," replied one of the sheriff's detectives. "We'll leave our guys on the outside. The parking lot has been shut down."

Marks stepped into the hall. "Yeah, Chief, what's up?"

Grey had been the Coloma Chief fourteen years now and, in all that time, had never had anything even close to this happen. Of course there had been homicides and the normal small town crime that colored every berg in the country. But having three otherwise healthy and by all appearances successful men commit suicide in his small town was beyond unusual. On top of that, the incredible story Marks had told earlier that day about the magic medals may have kicked this whole thing off.

'Okay," announced Grey, lighting his third cigarette of the morning. "Where are we at with this? The press is going to be crawling all over me in a couple of hours, maybe sooner. I'm already getting calls."

Marks shook his head. "All I know now, Chief, is that I have three dead from apparent suicide, suspects who may or may not be involved with the Robashaw death. Should have the toxicology on him this week. As far as motive for all this, right now all I have to go on is what Dale told me in his statement concerning the medals."

"Oh, that reminds me," announced the Chief reaching into his coat pocket. "Dale and his wife came down to the station this morning and gave me this." He handed Marks the blue velvet Crown Royal bag. "He said the medals were inside and that he would bring the diary and the rest of Robashaw's stuff down later this morning."

Mark's took the bag, feeling the heft of the Medallions inside. "What do you want to do with these, Chief? I mean I think this is something that needs to go to a higher authority."

Grey thought for a moment as he snuffed out the cigarette. "All right, here's what I want you to do. Under *no* circumstances," he grabbed Marks by the arm and led him further down the hall, "and I mean under *no* circumstances, are you to say anything about what you saw or what you were told about the medals by Dale. *Nothing.* Are we clear?"

Marks nodded. "You got it, Chief. I'll book this into evidence and…"

"No," interrupted Grey, "you lock this bag and anything else that Dale brings down to the station in the Narcotic's locker. I don't believe in magic medals or any other crazy horse shit but, just in case, I want this stuff under lock and key until I can figure out what to do with it or who to take it to. All right?"

Marks stuffed the bag into his coat pocket. "Sure. So you don't believe me, about what I saw?"

Grey shook his head. "I don't know what to believe, Jim. What I do know is that I have three dead guys in a hotel in my town, and my lead investigator is telling me all this is about some magic medals that make people disappear and fly. So, until I figure out some of this, I want you to stay quiet, investigate the dead, and let me try and get a handle on what is going on. Okay?"

Marks could see that Grey was just about at the end of his rope with all of this and way over his head. "Okay, Chief, I'll get it done."

Grey smiled, patting him on the shoulder. "All right, good. When Dale comes down to the station later, we will talk to him together. Okay?"

Marks nodded. "No sweat, Chief. We'll process this here and just start checking the boxes."

As Grey walked away, Marks told himself that he would, from this moment on, document every word anyone spoke to him about the medals. There was something far more powerful happening here than just three crazies killing themselves in Coloma, Michigan. He knew what he saw in the Dale's living room, and that alone was enough to kill for. Obviously, men dedicated to a cause, willing to kill themselves or anyone else that they viewed as a threat, was something off-the-scale dangerous and way beyond the pay-grade of this backwater town police detective and his nervous, chain-smoking Chief. He would be calling the FBI himself as soon as he cleared the scene. No matter what Grey said, he was moving this up the food chain as fast as he could. There was now thick blood in the water, and large predators were swimming in the dark.

Part Two

Dark Water

Chapter Seventeen

Clark had been nursing a beer for the last half-hour, doing everything he could think of to keep from walking outside, catching the Metro and going home. He had stayed at work late and at the Green Turtle even later. The bar, a DC landmark, was an easy walk from his office at the FBI. When he first started showing up to get a beer, he used the excuse that the food was good and it was close. Now, he neither needed nor made an excuse for showing up. He had a pain that would not go away until he had a good buzz. With regularity now, he counted on the liquor to chase the heavy memories into the haze.

As he sat in his customary booth near the back of the room, he watched the DC elite filter in and out. A full cast of actors, the "in your face" pretty women who stalked the halls of power in every Government organization - predators in four-inch heels and the heavy hitters, who laughed too loud, stood too close, and only kept secrets if the GS rating or clearance was high enough. Money was the vehicle but power was the fuel. If you mingled with the crowd of all the *cool* people, you could smell it.

Clark had killed all his dragons, sacrificing a marriage for the career. He had let the fires burn down from all the bridges he had torched and walked away from embers. He had been a rising star in the Albuquerque field office, the guy who hit all the shiny spots, someone who had been well on his way to bigger and better things and then one sunny afternoon, two years ago in June, when the pink sandstone canyons of the Sandia Mountains were brimming with wild juniper and green sage, he got a phone call. The call had been a lighting bolt out of the blue that had changed his perfect world forever. Thinking back over that day, an involuntary shiver ran down his back, bringing all the darkness to the surface.

He downed the last of his beer, pissed that it was taking more and more of it to dull the pain. The bar was getting loud as he slowly pulled on his coat and weaved his way through the crowd. He nodded to several of the people who worked on his floor, married agents looking for that secret thrill, the discreet encounter with the drunk, loud, and pretty things that he too had once pursued. Now, he wanted no part of it.

He stepped outside, feeling a refreshing nip in the air. The gusty wind made him roll up the heavy collar of his overcoat. The Metro was only a few blocks away and the walk would help him clear his head before he stepped onto the train. *DC - what a shit hole*, he thought, *nothing but climbers and killers, a good place to find the worst in careerism and wasted effort.* DC was not a city you warmed up to. The population was far too transient, coming and going with the tide like fetid political bilge water. The only community cohesiveness he found was in the local condo association out in Fredericksburg and the extended-stay residence hotels in Crystal City. Those were the cities full of people who were going someplace.

Since he had transferred from the New Mexico office he had not been right, right - meaning he always seemed to be carrying a low-grade fever, not enough infection to warrant a doctor but enough body discomfort to keep him slamming aspirin all day and booze at night. He woke up with body aches for no apparent reason and since he had stopped working out months ago, he knew that couldn't be the source. As he made his way down the steps to the metro he thought of the increasing difficulty he was having with concentration at work. Frequently his mind wandered off it to a thousand other places he would rather be and a thousand other things he would rather be doing. It was maddening.

Clark was convinced that they had done something to him, something that he was unable to fix and it was something that was getting worse. All of his adult life he had maintained a ridged, predictable routine over his health, marriage, and career. Now his health was slipping. Carol was long gone with that idiot Phil, the insurance salesman and his career with the FBI was hanging by a thread. As he stepped onto the train, he thought back to the day he got the news that he was being transferred to the Art Theft Unit in DC. *Art theft? Christ, if there were ever a backwater unit in which to end your career,* he thought, *this would be it.* The twelve agents assigned to the office were responsible for worldwide investigations involving painting thefts, fraud, and religious artifacts. He never did get a straight answer as to why he had been transferred especially since he knew little to nothing about art. *No, this had been done to warehouse him, get him out of the way. The case that had changed the trajectory of his career was the one in Albuquerque. That case had changed everything.*

Getting to his stop, he let the introspection fade. Hashing up what could have been did nothing to help him now. He was a professional law enforcement officer and would give whatever task he was assigned to a hundred percent of his effort. Nothing would change that. He had been with the bureau for sixteen years now and had every intention of riding it out till he hit twenty.

Besides, what else was a forty-seven-year-old ex-Marine with bad knees and only three hundred and twelve dollars in the checking account going to do? Standing at the top of the stairs, he tried to remember if he had any food in the apartment. Remembering that there were a couple of TV dinners left in the freezer, he headed down the street, weaving in and out of the large number of commuters heading home. He was lucky that his apartment was close enough to the office to walk. Most of the people who worked in the city commuted as much as an hour and a half each way, a ball busting way to end the day.

Stepping inside his apartment, he tossed the keys on the dining room table, part of his daily ritual. Carol had always gotten on his case about it, telling him in mock anger that the kitchen table was no place for a wad of keys. Tonight, he would give a year's pay just to hear her say it again. He found the TV dinner, dropped it into the microwave, and punched in the cook time just as his phone rang.

"This is Clark."

"Hey, Dave. This is Rodeo. Sorry to call you at home."

Clark sat down in an easy chair, the only real piece of furniture in the room besides the large screen TV. Rodeo Ramirez had been his supervisor for a year now, a decent guy in Clark's mind but not someone you would want to suit up with to take down a crack house full of mutants. He was a good tassels-on-the-shoes administrator, a guy who knew how to work the heavy hitters on the fourth floor without losing his nuts in the process. "Yeah, Rodeo, what's up?"

"Well, we just got a case that I think might be right down your skill set."

"Ah, okay. What skill set is that?"

Rodeo chuckled nervously. "Ah, you know, Dave. You have to admit you've been involved in some pretty weird shit."

"Not by choice, pard. The weirdness just seems to find me."

"Well, this one just came in and I think it might be something you would find interesting."

Clark knew where this was going. "I've already been assigned the case haven't I?"

Ramirez laughed. "'Fraid so, buddy. File is in your inbox. If it's any comfort, the assignment came from the top."

Clark pushed the recliner back and kicked off his shoes. "Who else is with me on this?"

"Hey, you know the old saying, *One Riot, One Texas Ranger*. One strange case - one strange Agent. You are the man on this one."

To Clark, the solo assignment meant that the case in question had the very real potential to go sideways and the shot callers wanted as little collateral damage as possible. Being assigned to a case by yourself was a bad omen.

"Okay," replied Clark rubbing his forehead, feeling the headache already setting in. "Where am I headed? Bermuda, maybe, Hawaii?"

Ramirez laughed. "Keep dreaming, brother. Nope, you're headed to Michigan, some small town called Coloma and, seeing that it's now late November, I would guess the weather there is downright balmy this time of year."

Clark thought for a moment, remembering the times he had gone through the Chicago area in the winter and the only word that came to mind to describe the experience was *miserable*. "When do I have to be there?"

"You're already gone, my friend. You've been booked out of Dulles tomorrow at ten and will get into South Bend by, let me see here, ah, twelve-thirty. According to the map, the town of Coloma is about a half hour drive from the South Bend airport. Should be fun. Keep your receipts."

"All right. Is there a POC in Coloma?"

"Hang on just a second. Okay, here it is. A detective by the name of Jim Marks, from the local PD is your POC. Anyway, Dave, all the info is in the file. Check in with me when you get to Coloma. Believe it or not, there are *a lot* of eyes on this one."

Clark laughed. "When are there *not* a lot of eyes on anything we do? Anyway, I'm on it. Anything else?"

"Nope. Just be safe. Lions, tigers, and bears -you know."

"Got it."

"Cya"

"Yep"

Lion's, tigers, and bears…. if he only knew.

Chapter Eighteen

Within the high walls of the Vatican sits the Casina Pio IV, an ornate, white marble building, better known as the Pontifical Academy of Sciences. Founded in 1603, the organization was apply named the <u>Academia dei Lincei</u> or the Academy of Lynxes. Its founding leader was none other than Galileo. Inside, the walls are covered with priceless paintings, frescos and tapestries, accouterment testifying to great wealth and power. On the second floor is a nondescript office, a room to which only a powerful few have access. It is home to the d'inchiesta Parlamentare or Select Committee. The Select Committee receives its mandates and directives from only the Pope himself, a straight-line-power matrix with no middleman, a level of absolute control that has existed for centuries. Julian De Parman had been voted to the Committee Chairman position for the last two terms. The board of Cardinals' vote had been unanimous both times.

De Parman was a massively built man of over three hundred pounds, a person who carried the mantle of the most powerful individual in Europe with an odd combination of indifference, intellect, and disdain. His lineage could be traced back to the most prominent families in Italy, a lineage that had always served as the keeper of secrets – world-changing secrets.

It was well known within Committee history that Julian's father had served an unprecedented three ten-year terms as chairman. He had been a man of astonishing intellect and equally astonishing ruthlessness and cruelty, attributes he had passed down to Julian in abundance. His calls were never ignored. His requests for meetings with Head of States always granted. To do otherwise was both foolish and dangerous. The d'inchiesta Parlamentare was not an organization you brushed aside. You did so at your own peril.

On this morning, like every morning at nine o'clock sharp, De Parman was meeting with the four other committee adjutants to discuss, strategize, and decide what action to take on a myriad of projects and initiatives currently facing The Committee.

"So, it's confirmed? We have lost three?" It wasn't so much a question but a statement, one of the unique ways De Parman communicated with his subordinates. He knew the answer to most of the questions he asked. Giving the other party a chance to answer was merely an annoying formality.

"Yes, that's correct," replied Mario Costa, the youngest of the five men now sitting around the small table in De Parman's office. De Parman had personally recruited him from the prosecuting attorney's office of the Italian Supreme Court.

De Parman slowly sipped his tea. "Where are the Medallions now?" he asked, his voice barely a whisper.

Costa handed the Chairman a newspaper clipping from the Harold Palladium, a Saint Joseph, Michigan newspaper. "As you can see, Sir, the suicides are mentioned in this article. The local police department in Coloma, Michigan, is handling the case. We know that a subject by the name of Preston Dale had the medals last. He evidently told the police of our team's inquiry, and we assume he gave them the Medallions. They should be in their evidence facility."

De Parman slowly set his teacup on the table. "All right, send in the Dragons. The intellectuals have failed again. Find the Medallions. I want them under our control within forty-eight hours, and I do not intend to lose any more of our people." He checked his watch. "I have a meeting with Senior Council day after tomorrow. I expect to give them a favorable report. Is that understood?"

Costa cleared his throat. "Sir, what about the remains of our people? What are your instructions?"

De Parman thought for a moment. "Their souls are in Paradise. I care nothing for the husks. The normal channels of recovery will be sufficient."

"Yes, sir. Very good."

"Gentlemen, if that's all," replied De Parman, "I have a meeting to attend."

All the men except Costa excused themselves and left the room. De Parman looked up from his notes, surprised to find the young officer still there. "Councilor?"

Costa thought for a moment. "Sir, I know you are aware of the possible consequences of utilizing the Dragons for this case."

De Parman sat back in his chair, as a slight look of amusement crossed his face. "Do you have a problem with the Dragons' methodology concerning these matters?"

Costa shifted in his chair. He was getting into dangerous territory and he knew it. "Well, sir, ah, it's just that.. this is going to take place in the United States. Maybe we should tread lightly. I would not like to see US Government involved in something we did."

De Parman smiled without humor. "Your trepidation is noted, Councilor. But I can assure you that the Dragons will accomplish what needs to be done. As far as the Americans are concerned, you should know by now that our reach is long and that we have friends there that are more then willing to help our cause. The Dragons are merely insurance. Is there anything else on your mind?"

Not wanting to generate further agitation, Costa slid his chair back and stood. "No, sir. I'm sure things will go as planned. I will notify the team leader myself."

The Chairman went back to his notes. "Thank you, Councilor," he replied without looking up. He sipped his tea as if no one else was in the room. Costa had been dismissed.

Walking out of the building, Costa still could not shake the feeling that the Chairman was making a mistake in his decision to send in the Dragons. The ranks were made up of experienced professional soldiers from the French Foreign Legion, British SAS, and German GSG9 and he found them to be heavy-handed and hard to control once they were given a directive.

They were men fluent in a myriad of languages and operational skill sets, evasive terminology for killing people as efficiently and as quickly as possible. The unit had been formed several years after World War Two, using foreign nationals as *plausible denial* for all the hard-edged, wet-work that The Committee needed to have done. There had been rumors of such a unit, controlled and operated from the Select Committee over the years, but nothing had ever been proven.

More people were about to die in this, thought Costa, and there wasn't a thing he could do about it. As he walked to his car in the parking lot, he thought about how bloody protecting the faith had become. Nothing would be left to wild interpretation or speculation. Only the Word and perceptions of the religious leadership would be heard, no matter what the price in lives, money, and/or blood. Driving away from the lot, he was once again thankful that he had not taken the oath of charity, forgiveness, and benevolence to man, attributes the priesthood demanded, pillars of character he had destroyed years ago.

Chapter Nineteen

"You did what?" shouted Grey from behind his desk. "Why in God's name would you call the god-dammed FBI on this without letting me know? Hell, this case is only twenty-four hours old! Jesus, you are really putting me into a bind on this, Jim."

Marks sat in the chair on the other side of the desk. "Chief, listen, the Medallions are something way over our pay grade. I mean this is really powerful stuff, and we are going to need help."

Grey sat back in his chair shaking his head. After a moment he reached into one of the desk drawers and pulled out Robashaw's diary. "Here, read some of this crap," he announced, tossing the book on the desk. "It's the ramblings of a lunatic. Dale and his wife brought it in this afternoon. The poor woman looked like she was about to have a heart attack. She was scared to death."

Marks picked up the book and thumbed through the pages. "Chief, all I know is what I saw. I think you need to see it too."

Grey thought for a moment. "Okay. All right. Let's get this over with." He bent down behind the desk and began spinning the dials on the large safe that sat under the desk. He pulled the Crown Royal bag from inside and tossed it onto the desk. "Here ya go, Jim. Show me."

"You mean right here? Right now?" questioned Marks, not sure what to do.

Grey stood up from behind the desk, his hands on his hips "C'mon Jim, I am tired of hearing about god-dammed magic medals. Let me see for myself. Make me a believer."

Slowly Marks reached across the desk and picked up the bag. "I'm not really sure what to do here, Chief."

"Well, according to Dale, you put the medal around your neck and fly to the moon and back," replied Grey sarcastically. "So let's see it."

Taking a deep breath, Marks took the gold medal out of the bag and carefully draped the chain around his neck. Half expecting to be blown through the roof, he sat on the edge of his seat.

Grey raised his arms. "I don't see you disappearing or flying, Jim," he announced smiling.

Marks looked down at the medal. "I don't know what's wrong." He thought for a moment, suddenly remembering the color of the medal Dale had been wearing at the house. "Okay, Chief, this is what you need to see." He took the gold metal off his neck and picked up the silver. "All right, this might be kind of a shock," he said standing up.

"I think I'll survive, Jim. Let's see the magic."

Daryl Grey had always held a pride in his ability to remain strong in a crisis, worldly when it came to matters of the heart, and generally unflappable when it came to making hard choices. But what he witnessed, there in his office, took him emotionally out of his skin. He felt himself go weak in the knees from shock and stunned disbelief as his lead detective suddenly vanished. "Holy Shit," gasped Grey, slowly sitting down. "You have got to be kidding me."

From Marks' point of view nothing had happened. He could still see his arms and legs and was almost ready to apologize for believing in the medals when Grey suddenly spoke up, his voice a fearful whisper. "Jim, Jim, are you there?

"I'm here, Chief," he replied, removing the silver medal. "Pretty amazing, huh?"

Grey sat silent, open mouthed, trying to comprehend what he had just seen. "I, ah, when is the FBI getting here?"

Marks smiled, laying the medal on the desk. "Should be here around two this afternoon."

Grey nodded, still stunned by what he had just seen. "Good, good, " he replied, slowly reaching over and picking up the silver medal as if it were a live grenade. "Holy Crap," he whispered.

****

Walking through the South Bend airport on his way to his rental car, Clark was still trying to digest the information he had read in Rodeo's case briefing. The Medallions supposedly were Kabala medals that had played an important ceremonial role in the early church. According to the report, the importance of the medals could not be overstated. Believed stolen by Nazis during World War Two, they were to be returned to the Vatican. To Clark, the trip appeared to be nothing more than a courier job. Any single rookie agent in the Art Crime Unit could have made the flight, picked up the medals, and flown back to DC. It seemed like a waste of experienced manpower. At least now he understood why Rodeo had only assigned one agent to the case. After finding his car in the Hertz lot he made a call to the office. He needed to ask about the last per-diem check that was short a hundred and seventeen dollars. This was the second time the check had been wrong and a hundred dollars was a hundred dollars. "Hi, Molly. This is Clark."

Molly Halverson was practically an institution at the Unit and to the FBI in general, having been the travel office supervisor in DC for the last twenty-three years. "Hello, Agent Clark. How are you today?"

Clark had never heard an unpleasant word come out of the woman's mouth. "I'm fine, Molly. Hey listen, I'm calling about a couple of things. Ah, my last two per-diem checks were about a hundred dollars off and I was wondering if I could get that straightened out. It's not a lot of money, but nowadays every penny counts."

"Sure. Just give me a minute to pull up your reimbursement record." He could hear her typing on the computer in the background. "Okay, yep, I see it. Looks like you're owed, ah, let's see… yep, looks like we need to get you another hundred and thirty-seven dollars. Sorry about that."

"Can you tell me why it was short?" he asked hitting the on-ramp to the freeway.

"Yes, they kicked the expense report back due to a lack of signature. You forgot to sign on the backside of the form. If you come by the office this afternoon, you can sign and I can resubmit the paperwork."

He merged onto highway-30 headed to Michigan. "Ah, I can't come into the office today. I'm on travel but should be able to come by in a day or so when I get back."

There was a pause on the phone. "Are you on vacation?"

"No, I'm in Michigan, well, on my way to Michigan. I'm on a case."

There was a second long pause. "Ah, Jim, how did you get to Michigan?" she asked.

"Excuse me?"

"Ah, I have no record of you getting a booking. Did you do it yourself? I know some of the guys do that."

"No, Rodeo called me at home last night and said I needed to get on the case today. I checked in at Dulles like I always do."

He could hear more typing in the background. "Huh, I don't see any flight information on your trip. And I don't see any reimbursement record for the ticket. Not sure how you got the ticket. Anyway, I'll call Rodeo and see what the deal is."

He couldn't say why but Molly's confusion about the trip sparked a pang of fear in him. "Okay, like I said, I'll be in a day or so to sign those forms."

"Okay, Jim. Have a safe trip. I'll get this sorted out."

"Bye."

"See ya."

Putting the phone back in his pocket, he fought the urge to call Rodeo to find out why his travel to Michigan had not been booked through the Travel Office. If there was one thing he had learned over his time working for the Art Crime Unit, it was that nobody moved, ate, or bought anything pertaining to work unless it crossed Molly's desk. It just did not happen. Seeing the blue "*Welcome to Pure Michigan* " sign on the side of the freeway, he came to the realization that if the Travel Office had no official record of him leaving DC, no one else would either.

Under normal circumstances, his paranoia would have been in check and he would have written off the whole travel office snafu as just a minor clerical error. But in memory of the Albuquerque affair, he automatically jumped to an assumption that something dark and dangerous was behind it all with a certainty that it was about to hit *him* with full force. Things had started off as benignly as this one had in that case, and then it had all turned into anything *but* ordinary. In fact, even though it had been over a year since the case, he was still having a hard time getting his head right about what had happened.

He realized he was now starting to check his rear view mirror more then normal, even going as far as pulling off onto the shoulder of the road several times just to let cars go by. Little did he know that an hour behind him, the sleek, white, GS-650 was leveling off at a comfortable cruising altitude of 37,000 feet on its second leg from Rome to Chicago's Midway Airport. The five men onboard dozed peacefully, their backgrounds and abilities in stark contrast to the current, hushed, and quiet environment of the jet. Sleeping Dragons should never be disturbed.

Chapter Twenty

Preston was in the basement when he heard the doorbell ring. Whoever was on the porch was pushing it continually, and it was incredibly annoying. "All Right! ALL RIGHT!" he shouted, coming up the stairs and walking across the living room. "Just a second." He opened the door and was surprised to see Officer Marks and the Coloma Chief of Police, Daryl Grey. "Ah, hello. What's the problem? I already took Robashaw's things down to the department. There is nothing here."

Grey raised his hands. "We're not here for that, Mister Dale. We're here to talk to you. Can we come in?"

Preston thought for a moment, almost asking if he needed a lawyer. "Ah yeah. C'mon in."

"Mister Dale, I'll get right to the point," announced Grey, taking a seat on the living room couch. "I have now seen, with my own eyes, what one of the medallions can do."

"Which one was that?"

Grey shook his head. "The silver medal, the one that makes a person invisible. Christ, I still can't believe what I saw."

"What happened?" asked Preston.

"Detective Marks here put the medal on and vanished, right there in my office."

Preston couldn't help but chuckle. "That's what I told you when we dropped them off. Try using the gold one if you want a *real* thrill."

Grey grew even more excited. "You see that's' what I want to talk about. Just exactly how does the gold one work?"

Preston thought for a moment. "Well, I read the diary about how Robashaw experimented with both medals, specifically how he discovered that the gold medal allowed him to fly."

Grey was practically on the edge of his seat listening. "So what did you do?"

Preston shifted in his chair. He had no idea where the conversation was going. Maybe this was some sort of a legal trap. Hopefully, it was just curiosity. Rolling the dice, he continued. "Well, I drove out to that big field out past Hagar Shore Road and Blue Star Highway. Once I saw that nobody was around, I put on the gold medal, took off running as fast as I could, and started to fly."

Grey shook his head. "Wow, what was that like? Was it hard? I mean, what went through your head?"

"All I can say, Chief, is that the more you do it, the more you *want* to do it. It's very addictive. Really incredible."

"How do you stop?" asked Marks.

"That's the really cool part," replied Preston. "No matter, how fast or how high you're flying, all you do is sit up and you settle right back down to the ground."

"Amazing. Okay, Preston," replied the Chief. "Can I call you Preston?"

"Sure."

"Here's the deal, Preston. As you can probably guess, this kind of thing is way past anything we have been involved with. So we have called in the FBI."

"Shit, the FBI," replied Preston, more than just a little alarmed. "Am I in trouble? Do I need to get a lawyer?"

"No, no," replied Marks. "They are just coming here to pick up the medals and to investigate this situation. I know they are going to want to talk to you. You're not in trouble. Just tell them how you got the Medallions and what you told us. There's no law against people flying."

"Ah, okay," replied Preston warily. "Hopefully I'm not getting charged with some Federal crime or something. What about the three guys and Robashaw's son that came here yesterday? What do I say about that?"

"Just tell them what you told us. Just tell them the truth," announced Grey standing. "They should be here around two this afternoon, a little over an hour from now. When they get here, I will bring them over and you can tell them what you told me. Okay?"

Preston thought for a moment. "Okay, but, Chief, would you do me a favor and not come back in a marked police unit? My neighbors are already jumpy enough."

"You got it, Preston," replied the Chief heading for the door, "and thank you for talking to us. We'll be back in about an hour."

As Preston shook hands and watched the men leave, he felt as if he had stepped out of his body and was watching events unfold without him having any control on the outcome whatsoever. It was a terrible feeling.

***

Due to chronic quirky legislative procedures throughout the state of Michigan, the I-30 freeway ends on a sweeping turn just west of the city of Saint Joseph. Clark followed the signs and after a two-mile drive on two lane surface streets, merged onto highway-94, a main artery in the state. By two o'clock that afternoon, he was sitting at Coloma's only stoplight. Finding City Hall, he pulled into the parking lot, still trying to figure out how a religious artifact highly sought after by the Vatican ended up here.

"Afternoon, Ma'am," announced Clark, stepping up to the reception counter. "I'm here to see a Detective Marks."

The middle-aged city clerk looked up from her desk. "And you are?" she asked flatly, having instantly sized him up as someone in trouble, another person coming with a problem for her detectives.

Clark held up his ID wallet containing his badge and credential. "Agent Clark, with the FBI." He never got tired of doing that. It always got people's attention and the clerk was no exception.

Immediately, the woman was out of her chair. "I will let him know that you're here," she replied, smiling and picking up the phone. "Jim, there is an FBI agent out here to see you." She said it loud enough for the other two younger women in the office to hear.

Moments later Marks came out of one of the room's side doors. "Agent Jim Marks, Coloma PD. Pleasure to meet you," he announced, shaking hands. "The Chief's office is back here. Follow me."

The first thing that struck Marks about the agent was his uncanny resemblance to the comedian Drew Cary. He wondered if anybody else picked up on the same thing.

"Chief, the FBI is here," announced Marks, stepping into Grey's office.

"Agent Clark," he replied shaking hands. After the initial small talk about the flight in and the drive from the airport, Grey pulled the bag containing the medals out of the safe and pushed them across the desk.

"Here's why we called you, Agent Clark. They are incredible."

Clark took the medals out of the bag. "So this is what all the fuss is about?"

Marks and Grey were both surprised by the comment. "Ah, Agent Clark, how much do you know about this case, if you don't mind me asking?" Marks asked, not sure if he was out of line with his question.

Clark put the medals back in the bag. "Well, only what I read in the brief from my office. The medals were taken from France by the Nazis. They are very important to the Vatican, and they very much want them back."

Marks looked over at Grey, not sure what to say. "So, you haven't been told anything about the medals themselves?"

"Well, nothing other than that they are priceless early church relics. Is there something more I need to know?"

Marks shifted in his chair uneasily. "Agent Clark, when I called your office in DC, I gave them some very specific information about these Medallions and the really strange things that have been going on since we have been in contact with them."

"Strange, like how?"

"Like three men committing suicide in a hotel in downtown Watervliet after possibly killing a forth man connected with the medals," interrupted Gray. "Right now, Agent Clark, we are hip deep in a possible murder-suicide investigation."

Clark was starting to feel the hair rise on the back of his neck. "Who were the men?" he asked, taking out a small note pad.

"Three Italian nationals. They killed themselves with cyanide in the Fairfield Inn in Watervliet." Clark looked up from his pad. "Cyanide...Why? What was going on?"

"Well, this is where it gets complicated. Evidently the three men went to the home of the guy who had the medals two days ago and demanded them. They threatened him and told him that they expected him to bring the Medallions to the hotel at nine AM the next day."

"Okay, I'm following you so far."

"Well, like I said, it now gets complicated. It seems that the son of the guy who originally had the medals came up here from Montana to talk to the current holder of the medals while the three Italian nationals were at the house here in Coloma."

"Wait a minute," interrupted Clark. "Where is the guy who *originally* had the medals?"

Marks shook his head. "He's dead, died from a stroke two and a half weeks ago over in Watervliet."

"Jesus, this is complicated," announced Clark, looking up from his notes.

"Hang on to your hat," replied Grey, lighting a cigarette. "You ain't heard nothing yet."

"Okay," continued Marks, leaning forward in his chair, "I never even knew the medals existed until two days ago when I was doing a neighborhood sweep near the location of the fatal car crash. At the scene, dead behind the wheel of a Budget rental car was a white, forty-one-year-old male by the name of Carl Robashaw. His home address was Hamilton, Montana."

Clark looked up from notes. "What was he doing here?"

"Like I said," continued Marks, "the older Robashaw died of a stroke while he was here. The son, who lives in Montana, found out that he had died in Watervliet, just a mile or so down the road, and he comes up. He finds out his father had been staying behind Preston Dale's home, and he pays a visit to get some kind of closure. Are you following me so far?"

"So far. Go ahead."

"All right. As near as we can figure, Carl Robashaw shows up at the Dale residence and wants to talk to the guy about his dad. Really bad luck on his part, because the three Italian guys showed up at the same time. There was some kind of confrontation, and Carl Robashaw wound up dead as a hammer behind the wheel of his car."

"Okay, how did you find all this out?" asked Clark.

"Anytime we have a fatal vehicle accident, I get a call - standard SOP. I was canvassing the neighborhood to see if anyone witnessed the fatal - five-mile-an-hour car crash. I contacted Preston Dale, who lives on the street where this all went down. When I first made contact with him, he said that he did not know anything about the crash but as I was getting ready to leave the scene, he made a spontaneous statement about Robabshaw, the three Italians, and the Medallions."

Clark thought for a moment. "Okay, let's go back. How did this, ah, Preston Dale guy get the Medallions?"

"Evidently, the old man, Darcy Robashaw, had some sort of injury and was camped out behind Dale's residence. Dale found him out there in the woods and called an ambulance. As they are loading the old man up to take him to the hospital, he gave Dale a knapsack containing the medals and some personal papers for him to hang on to until he could get back. The next day the old man dropped dead from a stroke before he could leave the hospital."

"Wow, you really can't make this stuff up, " replied Clark.

"Hang on, it gets better. A couple days go by, Dale hadn't heard anything from Robashaw and he went to the hospital. He found out the old man had died. He went back to his house and started going through the bag to see if there was any contact information, next of kin, stuff like that. That's when he found the medals."

Clark sat back in his chair. "Okay, I think I now know how Dale got the medals. But who are these Italian guys and how do they know about the Medallions?"

Grey spoke up for the first time. "We don't know who these guys are, other than being Italian nationals. As far as why they are here - once I tell you what the medals can do, that will probably answer *that* question."

"All right, Chief. What's so special about the Medallions?" questioned Clark.

Grey looked at Marks warily, slowly shaking his head. The silver medal makes you invisible and the gold medal lets you fly." He let out a heavy sigh, still having a hard time believing what he had just said.

Clark looked at Grey and smiled. "Guys, what's going on here? This is a joke, right?"

Marks reached over and picked up the bag. "Agent Clark, I am going to show you something. It's the only way I am going to be able to convince you that the Medallions are far more important then anything you can imagine." He pulled the silver medal out of the bag. "Brace yourself. This may be a bit shocking."

Chapter Twenty-One

Tanner Sims cared little for the church and even less for the trinkets they so desperately chased around the world. He didn't believe in things he could not see nor tolerated very well those who did. He had been a professional soldier for twenty years and in all that time had never seen a miracle of divine intervention other than his own survival of countless operations within the ranks of the British SAS, Northern Ireland, Iraq, Afghanistan, and Africa. For Sims, blood was blood, and he did not care what color the person was who had spilled it. Death looked and smelled the same no matter what part of the planet it decided to visit.

He had never made this much money in the past for doing what he did best. He had never had the kind of shadowy political juice he now enjoyed, the quiet approval of men in positions of power, men who green-lightened the kind of operations that produced results, even if it was for just a select few. *Right, wrong - who gives a shit*, he thought walking up to the rental car counter. As long as the money stayed this good, he would do their bidding - do the hard-edged things that most would not do regardless of how good the cash offer.

Because he had grown up poor, the son of a shipping clerk, living on the bare-knuckle west side of Manchester, England, had marked him deep and early in life. Fistfights had been common, bloody beat downs by those stronger, meaner and bigger had been a part of everyday life for a small kid in that culture. By nine, he had lost one of his front teeth after being kicked in the face twice. By twelve, he had suffered broken ribs, a broken jaw, and a fractured wrist after being pushed down a flight of stairs. It had continued until he was able to hit back even harder, his punches landing cleaner. By sixteen, he was breaking other people's jaws with a wicked left hook that he had picked up at the Manchester United Boxing Club downtown.

By eighteen, he had put on twenty pounds of muscle and gained enough street sense to get him killed or put in prison for the rest of his life. He became a thumb breaker for a small group of wanna-be gangsters who ran numbers and a bit of ditch-weed pot in his neighborhood. It had been only a matter of time til his number was up and he knew it, having seen several of his friends beaten to death by rivals, stabbed, hit by cars, or ruined by drink or drugs. Having just enough sense to see the handwriting on the wall, he had joined the Army and never looked back.

Now at forty-four, an age when the phone on the dark side of special operations rang less and less, he found himself in the employ of one of the most powerful societies in the world, an organization that had sent him and his equally dangerous teammates to South Bend, Indiana, chasing another trinket. After picking up both rental cars, Simms stepped away from the team in the parking lot and made a call.

"Yeah, Simms here. We are in the area. How do you want this played?"

"The Medallions will be in the care of an FBI agent by the name of Clark. He is at the Coloma PD now to pick up the medals. Find him. Retrieve the Medallions and bring them back here. This needs to be cleaned up and quickly. Spare no effort."

"Yes, Sir. What about the agent and any witnesses?" questioned Simms.

The line was silent a moment. "Agent Clark has been under a tremendous amount of stress lately. I believe a massive heart attack will solve all of our loose ends and stress. As far as a witness goes, I believe a thorough cleaning is in order. This is far too important."

"Yes, Sir, I understand."

"Mister Simms…"

"Yes, Sir?"

"Make sure this is as clean as possible. The waters are all ready murky enough. Do we understand each other?"

"Yes, Sir. Perfectly. Is there anything else?"

The line went dead. "Evidently not, " he mumbled, putting the phone in his pocket. "Yo, let's go," he said to the men standing around the rental cars. "Got about a thirty minute drive. Follow me."

***

Preston had just sat down in his living room when the doorbell rang, followed by a heavy knock. He looked out the front window and saw the unmarked police unit sitting in the driveway. Opening the door, he saw the Chief, Marks, and a third man he had not met before.

"Hello, Preston. We said we would stop by later to talk. Oh, and this is Agent Clark from the FBI. Can we come in?"

"Sure, come in."

Clark sat down on the sofa. "Well, I have to say .... I have never been interrogated by the FBI," Preston announced nervously as he took a seat in the easy chair across from Clark.

Clark smiled, taking out his small note pad. "No interrogation here, Mister Dale. I just wanted to clear up a few things. Okay? Thank you for your cooperation."

"No problem. Anything I can do to help."

"Great, Mister Dale, I…"

"Call me Preston," he interrupted.

"Okay, Preston. I want you to know that the Chief and Detective Marks have given me a demonstration of the silver medal."

"Pretty wild, huh?"

"To say the least," replied Clark. "I really think that the Medallions are far more powerful and possibly dangerous than we can imagine."

"Really, how so?"

Clark looked over at the Chief and back at Dale. "Preston, when you first found the Medallions in Robashaw's knap sack, what did you do with them?"

Preston had been dreading this moment but was now prepared to suffer the consequences. "I put the silver medal on, walked into McDonald's here in town and stole 80 dollars out of the till," he said softly. "I really feel shitty about taking the money. I really do. I, ah, I'll pay it back. I promise, I...."

"It's okay," chuckled Clark, holding up his hands. "Take it easy. Hell, I might have tried the same thing. No, Preston, what I am getting to is did you injure anyone while using the medals? Be honest with me. Okay?"

Preston, signed with relief and shook his head. "No, absolutely not." He left out the part about scaring three colors of shit out of the neighbor kids. "No, I would never hurt anyone."

"Good," replied Clark smiling, "Now another question. You told Detective Marks and Chief Grey that you also used the gold medal. Is that correct?"

Preston smiled. "Sure did. I read in Robashaw's diary about how he learned to fly so I did the same thing. I'm a writer, and even I don't have the words to describe how it feels."

"How many times would you say you used the gold metal to, ah, fly?"

Preston thought for a moment. "Twice, no, three times. The last time I flew to Iowa."

Clark looked up from his pad. "Excuse me?"

Preston smiled. "Yeah, no shit. I flew to Iowa and back."

"You flew to Iowa?"

"Yep."

"Do you know if anyone saw you flying to Iowa?"

"No, I doubt it. It was late in the afternoon, and, when I flew back, it was almost dark. Had a hell of a time finding my truck; the neighborhoods look a lot different from the air."

Marks had to laugh. The conversation was so ridiculous that he was still having a hard time getting his mind around it. "Sorry guys," he said, shaking his head. "It's just the way he said it. Struck me as funny, that's all."

"Well, guys, I have to tell you that I think this could get real serious very quickly," replied Clark. "Preston, who else knows about the medals?"

"Ah, just me and my wife. Oh ..wait... I showed them to a history professor at the local college. Cannot remember her name."

"Is that everyone? There's no one else that knows about the Medallions?"

Preston shook his head. "No one. I've kept this to myself."

Clark checked his watch. "Okay, Preston, I just have one last question. Did Robashaw tell you where he got the medals?"

"No, when I first saw him in the woods, he was pretty banged up. We made some small talk, and then I called the ambulance. That's the last I saw him. I never knew he had the medals until I looked in his knapsack."

Clark wrote down a few more notes. "I think I have everything I need, Chief. Unless you have any more questions for Preston, I'm done."

Grey shook his head. "No, I think that will do for now."

As the men stepped outside and headed to the car, Clark turned to see Preston watching them leave through the living-room window. He nodded to him before sliding into the back seat of Grey's unmarked car. "Guys, I have to make a phone call. I think we are going to have problems."

"What kind of problems?" questioned Grey, backing the car out of the driveway.

Clark stared out the window as the middleclass neighborhood slowly rolled by. "Bad ones," he mumbled to himself. "Real bad."

Chapter Twenty-Two

"Costa." He picked up the call on the second ring.

"Yes, sir," replied Sims. "We are just now coming into Coloma. Do you have any information about where this agent is staying?"

Costa opened the file. He had been waiting for this call. "Mister Sims, I understand that you called the Chairman earlier today."

"Yes, sir. Wanted to see if he had any other instructions."

"Mister Simms, please do not call the Chairman in the future. I am in operational control of this case, and I would appreciate it very much if you would not jump the chain of command."

"Sorry about that. I didn't think it would be a problem."

"Well, it is a problem. The Chairman is not to be bothered with the particulars of this case. The only thing he needs to hear is that you have the Medallions and are bringing them back to Rome."

"I understand."

"I hope you do, Mister Sims. I am counting on knowing that you will call me directly as this operation continues. Now, as far as where the agent is staying, I will get that information to you within the hour. At that point, locate the agent and keep him under surveillance. I am forwarding information on *Stone Gate* to you. Clark was deeply involved with that operation, and I'm sure it will be helpful."

"Yes, sir. I will wait for your call."

****

Many times over the years, De Parman, the Chairman, had been in the Bishops' office, an impressive place with mahogany paneling, vaulted ceilings, and priceless artwork adorning the pale blue walls. A large, nearly life size stature of Saint Francis of Assisi stands in the corner of the room, charging the atmosphere with a spiritual reverence that makes visitors speak in whispers. The Bishop had left a message with his priest's aide that he would be late with a request for De Parman to wait in his office. The Bishop arrived out of breath, having walked from the Pope's apartment back to his office. "My apologies, Mister Chairman," he announced, sitting down behind his desk. "Thank you for waiting. Can we get you some tea?"

"I'm fine, Your Eminence. Thank you."

The Bishop nodded and lit a cigarette. De Parman had always found clergy smoking off-putting, especially in someone of the Bishop's stature.

"Sorry for the cigarette, but my office is one of the few places I can still smoke. We are all becoming more like the health fanatics every day."

De Parman smiled slightly. "How can I help you, sir?"

The Bishop nodded, blowing a lung full of smoke toward the ceiling. "One of the things I like about you, Chairman - you get to the point of the issue or, as the Americans say, you cut to the chase."

"I know you are a busy man, Your Eminence. I would not want to waste your time."

The Bishop snuffed out the cigarette and sat back in his chair. "Which is why I asked you to come by my office. I need to know where we stand on the Medallions?"

The Chairman opened his black leather-bound notebook. "I have been informed that the Medallions were turned over to the American FBI. I have dispatched the Dragons to retrieve them and expect to have them in route to Rome within twenty-four hours."

The Bishop thought for a moment, keeping a steady gaze on the Chairman. "I know I don't have to tell you the incredible significance of the Medallions to the church - do I?"

"No, Your Eminence. I understand their importance. That is why I dispatched the people that I did. They are individuals more than capable of completing the task."

"Ah, this is no mere task, Mister Chairman. Do you know what the Medallions really are - why they are so important?"

De Parman thought for a moment, not sure where the Bishop was going with his questions. He always hated these left-handed lectures from men like the Bishop, men who rarely said what they meant, men whose careers within the Church hierarchy lived and died on innuendo and political warfare. "I know that the Medallions carry a certain kind of mystical power. I know that they are very old, I assume from the time of Christ."

"You are correct, if not understated, Mister Chairman. The Medallions are not from this world. And I say that in all candor."

"Is there something in particular you need me to do, Your Eminence?"

The Bishop got out of his chair and walked over to the large window that looked over the Fountain of the Sacrament garden. "Chairman, do you know how many sets of medals there are?"

"It is my understanding that there are twelve sets. The set in the states is the last of the group."

The Bishop turned from the window. "That is incorrect, Mister Chairman. We currently have twelve sets locked securely in our vaults."

De Parman suddenly came to a jarring realization. "So, you're saying that the twelve sets, from all twelve apostles, have been secured?"

"Have been for decades, Mister Chairman. But the thirteenth set is very special. They have a value far beyond human comprehension."

"Thirteen sets - thirteen men in the upper room," whispered De Parman. The Bishop walked back to his chair and sat down. "Precisely, Mister Chairman. Everyone in the Christian world knows who the thirteenth man in the upper room was."

De Parman was stunned by the enormity of what was being said. "You're telling me that this set of Medallions were worn by…"

"Yes, by Jesus Christ himself."

****

Clark was already punching in the phone number when they arrived at the Coloma Police Department. "Gentlemen, if you don't mind," he said from the back seat, "I have to make this call. I'll meet you inside in a minute."

"No sweat," replied Grey, handing him the keys. "Just lock it when you're done."

A second later, Rodeo Ramirez answered the line. "Agent Ramirez. Can I help you?"

"Hey, Boss. Clark here."

"Hey, Clark. How's it going out there?"

"Well, not too good there, Rodeo. It seems that this is a whole lot more complicated than just picking up a couple of church relics."

"Complicated? How so?"

Clark was working hard to control his anger. "To begin with, there is a murder/suicide investigation going on that seems connected to the medals with a real possibility that a fourth murder is rolled up in this. On top of that, three of the dead are foreign nationals. What's going on, Rodeo? Why wasn't I told anything about this."

"You were told just what you needed to be told, Clark. Secure the Medallions and bring them back to DC. That's your job - nothing more."

"Hey, listen to me a minute. First off, I'm not a high-priced errand boy. Secondly, these medals are already getting people killed and I know why."

"You know, Agent, you're riding right on the edge of insubordination, and..."

"Don't even start with that shit, Rodeo. There is something really heavy going down out here, and you put me right in the middle of it."

"What are you talking about? Right in the middle of what?"

"Well, for one thing, how is it that the travel office doesn't know I'm here, Rodeo?"

"What are you talking about? I made the arrangements myself. This is a sensitive case. I'm taking extra precautions. What's your problem?"

"Precautions against what? You know more about this case than you're telling me. What's really going on here?"

"Agent Clark, as your supervisor I am telling you to retrieve the medals and stand by for a government jet to pick you up in South Bend tomorrow. I will text you the arrival time. Is that understood?"

"I understand what you're saying, but there is…."

"That's enough, Clark," interrupted Ramirez. "Be at the airport with the medals tomorrow. End of discussion."

A block-and-a-half away, Simms and the other men sat in rental cars in a closed bowling alley parking lot. They had a clear line-of-sight to the Police department parking area and had seen Agent Clark leaving one of the parked units, slamming the door angrily.

"Look's like our guy isn't very happy," chuckled Simms, looking through the small set of binoculars.

The team member sitting beside him, an ex-SAS operator in his early fifties who had served with Simms for years, sipped his coffee. "How ya want to do this, mate?"

Before Simms could answer, his cell phone rang. "Yeah."

A voice on the phone said, "He should have the medals today. He's been told to be at the South Bend airport tomorrow. You should make your move as soon as you can."

Simms thought for a moment. "Listen, mate, I know you're just trying to help, but you're not on the ground; I am. We will get the objects when we have the advantage. Thanks for the information. You'll be contacted when we are successful. ...Thank you." He ended the call and dropped the phone back into his coat pocket. "Fuckin wanker," he mumbled.

The other team member laughed. "You know, Boyo, you shouldn't piss off the FBI like that."

Simms brought the binoculars up, checking the now empty parking lot. "FBI, my ass, bunch of shit-birds. Got no use for em."

Fifteen hundred miles away, Rodeo Ramirez, section leader to the FBI Art Crime Unit, punched in the overseas' number and waited for the call to be answered. "Good evening, sir. This is Ramirez. I wanted to let you know that I have ordered my agent to secure the medals and to be at the airport tomorrow afternoon."

"Very good, Agent Ramirez. My team is already there," replied Costa.

"Yes, I know. I just talked to them. Sir, are you confident they can handle this?"

"Agent Ramirez, I have the utmost confidence. Please stay focused on your part of the operation."

"Yes, sir. I understand."

"Very well, Mister Ramirez. Please remember that we are paying you a very large sum of money for results, results we fully expect."

"Yes, sir. This will go smoothly."

"Very good, Agent. Please keep me informed."

"Yes, sir. Goodbye."

Ramirez turned off the phone, looking at the small gold crucifix and chain that hung from his desk lamp. He wasn't just doing this for the money, he told himself as he gently touched the cross. He was doing this because it had to be done. Over the last two years he had taken hundreds of thousands of dollars from The Committee, collecting and diverting many sensitive art works for the church, works and relics deemed too important to go through the normal slow-moving evidence process and government channels. No, he wasn't doing this for the money; he was doing God's work. At least that's what he told himself so he could sleep at night. Lately, even that was wearing thin.

Chapter Twenty-Three

"So, how do you want to proceed with this? Is the FBI going to take the case?" asked Marks, pouring a cup of coffee.

Clark sat down in one of the office chairs in Grey's office, trying to think of an answer. He had caught Rodeo in a lie, and that realization alone had shaken him deeply. Something was going on behind his back in this case, something very dangerous. "Well, I'm not really sure how I should proceed with this," he replied stalling. "Not sure what direction to go…"

"Not sure what direction?" announced Grey surprised. "If you are having a problem trying to find a starting point on this case, how about starting with the fact that these medals allow people to do things that are *supernatural,* for lack of a better word."

"That is exactly my dilemma, Chief. What to do with the information I have," replied Clark.

Grey sat down behind his desk, visibly agitated. "You're the FBI, for Christ's sake. Isn't there a unit in the bureau that handles…you know, this kind of weird…?"

"X-files?" interrupted Clark, smiling.

Grey nodded. "Yeah, you know, stuff that's off the charts of known reality. Surely you have some kind of team or something that looks into things like this?"

"Chief, I really wish we did. I would drop this case in their lap in a second. Unfortunately, I'm it."

Marks handed him a cup of coffee. "So what's next?" he asked, sitting down. "What do we do?"

Pondering the question, Clark knew there was no easy answer to the question. The Medallion's were far and above anything he had ever dealt with before. In the wrong hands, or even in the right hands, the medals could change society dramatically. The power to manipulate was a temptation few, if any, men could resist.

"What I will do is secure the Medallions and then head back to DC. There are people, experts, that can give me a definitive answer on what these things really are."

"Good," announced Grey slapping his desktop. "The sooner those things are out of my city the better."

"Chief, I don't think taking the medals out of the city will solve our problem." replied Marks, easing back in his chair.

"Why? If they aren't here, they are not a liability."

Clark shook his head. "Jim is right, Chief. If the people who sent the three foreign nationals want the Medallions bad enough to send them here, they are bound to send more. They've proven that they are willing to kill for them."

Grey sat back and lit a cigarette. "So what do you think?"

"I'm going to go over what we have so far, make a few calls, and let you know. I am scheduled to fly out tomorrow."

"Tomorrow?" questioned Marks. "You just got here?"

"Jim, I was just sent here to pick up the Medallions. I had no idea you folks were involved in a possible homicide investigation."

"So what do you suggest?"

"Go ahead and conduct your investigation into the suicides and send me the information when you get it. In the meantime, I will start a case file on all of it and send it up my chain of command."

Grey thought for a moment. "All right. Sounds good. Thanks for you help, Dave. We'll get this moving from our side. He slid the Crown Royal bag across the desk. "Here you go."

"You'll also want this." Marks handed him Robashaw's diary. "Pretty interesting reading. Amazing actually."

****

A block and a half away from the police department parking lot, Simms and his partner sat in their car watching the lot. "You know this guy has been involved in some pretty scary shit," mumbled Simms's partner, thumbing through the thick file. "Especially this *Stone Gate* Business."

"Yeah, I know," replied Simms. "We need to play this pretty tight. After reading what took place in New Mexico, I don't think our boy gets shook up about too much."

The operator closed the file. "You think he'll play ball?"

Simms raised a small set of binoculars. "Counting on it."

By six-thirty that evening, Clark had cleared the PD, checked into his room, and ordered a pizza. He was exhausted and was already dreading the flight back to DC and the inevitable confrontation with Rodeo. He lay down on the bed and kicked his shoes off while dumping the medals out of the bag. The Medallions were beautiful. The workmanship in the inlay was incredible. Their beauty alone was enough to cause a man to become entranced.

As he examined the Medallions he could not shake the odd, yet very real feeling that he was a trespasser, someone who should not be in the possession of such beautiful objects. A knock at the door drew him from the feeling, and he quickly stuffed the medals back in the bag. "Hang on," he announced, getting off the bed. "Be right there." He pulled out his wallet, retrieving a twenty to cover the pizza and tip.

Ignoring all of his normal situational awareness standards as it applies to blindly opening a hotel room door, he unlocked the flip latch and opened the door without looking through the peephole. Stunned, he suddenly found himself looking at four men he had never seen before. Within a heartbeat, the door was shoved open, and he was kicked in the chest, the blow knocking him to the floor. In shock and trying to catch his breath, he found the attackers on him, zip-tying his hands and ankles. He was hooded and then picked up and thrown onto his back on one of the beds. In only seconds, he had been incapacitated. Just as he was about to shout out, a sledgehammer blow to the stomach silenced the scream. In agony, with his hands secured behind his back and his ankles bound, he curled into a fetal position, trying to get air back into his lungs.

A voice from the darkness was now at his ear. "Breathe, mate. Breathe. Stay quiet, and we'll let you keep breathing. Okay?" The accent was British.

"I'm an FBI agent, you son-of-a-bitch," he moaned. A second heavy blow to the kidneys nearly made him pass out.

"Oh, we know who you are, Agent Clark. Now stop being a prick and settle down. If not, I will pound on you all night. Okay?"

Clark fought through the pain. "What do you want?" He said as he was roughly jerked back into a sitting position on the bed, his back against the headboard.

"Okay, now that we have your attention, Agent Clark, I am going to fill you in on why we are here and why it involves you."

"Take this hood off so I can see."

The voice chuckled. "No chance, mate. Protocol and procedures need to stay in place. Besides, you need to focus on what I am saying instead of trying to memorize my beautiful face. I know how you FBI boys are. Now, here's the deal. We are taking the Medallions that you have so faithfully retrieved for us. We will also take that diary off your hands." He leaned close. "The next thing I need you to hear is that we know all about your adventures in New Mexico. I believe *operation STONE GATE* should ring a bell."

Instantly, Clark felt a bolt of terror rip through his body. *Stone Gate* - the words were almost as powerful as a punch.

"Ah, I can see by your reaction that they really worked you over during your re-education. That must have been a nasty bit of business."

"Who are you people?" gasped Clark, slowly getting his breath back. He could feel the weight of someone sitting down on the bed.

"Here's the deal, Agent. I would really like to stay and talk with you but my associates and I have to be going. What I will leave you with though is this. I am just a messenger, but my superiors, they, would very much like to talk to you about *Stone Gate*. I've read part of the file myself, and it is very interesting reading. I am leaving the contact phone number on the desk here. It's in your best interest to call."

Clark struggled against the ties. "You really think I am going to cooperate with you after this?"

The voice leaned close. "Ah, I really do, Mister Clark," he whispered. "You see, I think you need to know that your boss, your direct line supervisor, and his boss sold you out. They told us where you were and what you were picking up."

"You're lying," replied Clark angrily. Even as he said it, he instinctively knew it was true. This was supposed to happen. It had been a set-up from the beginning.

"Not a lie, my friend. Your supervisor's name is Rodeo Rodriquez, the AIC of the Art Crimes unit. Just talked to him last night. So you see, Agent Clark, in a strange way, I am your friend. I'm the only person in your world right now that is telling you the truth."

Clark thought for a moment. These are pros. If they had wanted him dead, he would have been there two minutes ago. "Why the rough stuff, asshole?" he asked, trying to get any type of information.

The voice laughed. "That's really good, tough guy. Seriously, would you have given me the medals if I walked up and asked you for them?"

"No, not a chance in hell. So what's next?" he asked. His fingers were growing numb, the zip ties cutting into flesh. "This is just some half-assed robbery?"

He felt the man get off the bed. "What's next? We are leaving with the medals. I think we have taken up enough of your time. We are not thieves, Agent Clark. We are the ones who return things to their rightful owners. I am going to leave a very sharp knife on the bathroom sink for you to use to get the zip-ties off. Try to not cut yourself. Suddenly, Clark felt a small needle jab just above his knee. "Here is something to help you sleep. Should wear off in about three hours."

"I'm going to find you, pal," replied Clark calmly. "I'm a Federal Agent. You're not going to get away with this shit." He could hear the men moving around in the room.

"You know, first off, it's really kind of silly to be making threats while you're under that hood tied up like a Christmas turkey. Secondly, Agent, surely you realize that your career is pretty much over. You have been discarded. Call the number. Get some answers. Remember - you have no friends at the FBI."

"Wait a minute," mumbled Clark. The drug was beginning to take him under as he heard the room door close. Less than a minute later, he was unconscious.

Walking down the hallway toward the exit, Simms made the call. "We have the items. Heading home now."

"Very good, Mister Simms. Your transport is waiting in South Bend. Well done."

****

An hour later, the rental cars had been dropped off and the sleek white Gulfstream Four was thundering down the South Bend Indiana Airport runway on it's way back to Italy. As the plane gently banked on its course correction east after take off, Simms pulled the Medallions out of the bag. The craftsmanship and weight were impressive. Even in the dimly lit cabin, the medals glistened, the engraved facets picking up the muted light. Holding them up by the chain, he downed the last bit of whisky. "Beautiful," he mumbled. "Beautiful."

Chapter Twenty-Four

In Washington DC, at the National Security Agency or NSA, just off Carlton street, stands a nondescript four-story brick building, a place of hidden yet incredible power, where every electronic signal from automotive black boxes to computer and cell phone traffic is captured, analyzed, stored, and then used in whatever manner the real government sees fit. In any official plot maps or NSA asset memorandums, the facility is simply known as "annex 7." No administrative flow chart of supervisors or individuals working out of the building exists. It is a totally paperless government facility, the only one in the United States. Being found with any kind of writing material inside the building is a severely punishable offense. Access to the site is gained through the parking garage off Halifax Avenue a half a block away. At street level, a proximity card opens a grey, unmarked elevator door, which in turn leads to a long, brightly lit hallway two floors below, followed by a barred electronic gate and two armed NSA police officers.

Only after the visitor is wanded, all electronic devices are removed and stored, and a retinal scan performed is the visitor allowed entrance. The facility is manned twenty-four seven with roving patrols, redundant CCTV, and a myriad of monitoring devices and anti-intrusion systems throughout the facility. It is the most heavily guarded building in Washington DC.

It is an operations and intelligence apparatus that the general pubic has never seen nor heard of. It is also where the words "*Stone Gate*" were picked up within the data blade servers by a word matrix program that filters catch words and phrases. It was picked up on the high frequency wireless data recorder used for cell phone traffic coming in from Europe. This system alerts to generic words such as *bomb, guns, attacks, jihad,* along with a classified list of all past and current intelligence operations. The data is routinely captured and transferred to NSA analysts who run the data against current open and closed investigations. Names are compared along with word matrix files from the FBI, CIA and DIA. Everything that moves through cyber space is seen or touched by this system. Ron Stacy was the first field analyst at the main NSA office to see the *Stone Gate* references the next morning. The file had been encrypted as highly sensitive and carried a *Yankee White* security classification; a tag far above Top Secret/SCI. Few people, outside the President and certain members of Congress, had this security clearance designation.

According to the report, the call mentioning *Stone Gate* had originated from a cell phone in Italy and had been received by a mobile cell in Michigan. In his office Stacy ran a direct designator program on the Italian call, a program that triangulates all cell phone repeater signals worldwide, pinpointing within ten yards the place of the call. As the data on his screen rolled up the coordinates and the map location of the originating signal, he immediately picked up the in-house phone. "Yeah, this is Stacy. I just ran that flash information on *Stone Gate* we got yesterday."

On the other end of the line was E.J Briggs, the new AIC at the Agency, a retired sixty-three-year-old Army two-star, a no nonsense by-the-book administrator who had the reputation of weeding out bureaucratic dead wood. DC was full of GS 15 burnouts that did nothing but clog the system and drain Government Grievance offices all over town. "What did you come up with?" he asked, easing back in his chair.

Stacy checked the data again. "First time something like this has come out of here, and I've checked it three times now."

"Where's it coming from?"

"Sir, it's coming from the Vatican."

There was a pause on the phone. "I'll be right down," replied Briggs.

****

By eight o'clock that same morning eighteen hundred miles away, Clark sat in a rental car in the parking lot of the Coloma Police Department waiting for Detective Marks to arrive. It had taken him a full two hours to wake up after being drugged and another hour to get out of the zip-ties. The little fingers on both of his hands were still numb from the painful constriction.

Clark had not called Rodeo or anyone else that morning. His mind was still reeling at the fact that his own had betrayed him. There was nothing they could say that would cool the rage that had started to build. He had spent the rest of the sleepless night and early morning hours trying to figure out a strategy.

An involuntary shudder ran down his back as he remembered the feeling of absolute helplessness and vulnerability at being subdued and tied up. He had felt that only one time before in his life, a feeling he had vowed to never experience again. New Mexico had broken him, had taken him right down to the core of what he was. It had changed his view of where and who he was in the world, and now this incident brought it all back in a terrible rush. Feelings he had worked to suppress and forget almost to the point of blood were back. Worse yet, they had been brought back by people he trusted, men he knew and respected.

The voice was right; he no longer had friends in the FBI, not after last night. It was eight fifteen when he saw Marks pull into the parking lot, closely followed by Chief Grey. Evidently the men had had breakfast together. He would have to play this one close, he thought getting out of his car. He had to find out if either man was involved with last night. Having been an investigator for most of his adult life, spotting a lie would not take long. As he walked across the parking lot, he recognized that his only fear at this point was what he would do if he found it.

He caught up with Marks just before he walked into the back of the building. "Hey Jim."

"Morning, Dave," he replied, holding the door open. "C'mon in. Chief is in his office. What time is your flight?"

They walked into Grey's office. The Chief was on the phone talking to a business owner about clearing out a blocked driveway. To Clark the men seemed completely at ease, acting normal. If they had been involved with his assault, they were hiding it well. Grey nodded and held up his hand indicating he would be off the phone in a moment. Clark sat down in one of the office chairs, trying to figure out what he was going to say.

"Sorry, guys. Part of my job involves smoothing feathers," he said hanging up the phone. "Morning, Dave. How was your night in our big city?" he asked smiling.

"Well, not so good, Chief." He sighed. "The medals are gone. Just after I got back to the hotel, four guys showed up at my room. I thought it was the pizza delivery guy and opened the door. They rushed in and flex cuffed and hooded me. They took the medals and the diary, hit me with some kind of sedative and left."

Both Grey and Marks sat open mouthed in stunned surprise. "You have got to be shitting me?" announced Grey, looking as if he were about to cry. "What the hell is going on around here?"

"Why didn't you call us?" questioned Marks, still in shock. "We would have had a unit there in five minutes or less!"

"Honestly, guys, I don't know who to trust after this," replied Clark. "I haven't even called my office yet."

Marks was on his feet. "You think we had something to do with it, Dave?"

"Like I said, I don't know who to trust. There were only four of us who knew about the medals."

"So you are saying you suspect us?" replied Grey. "Furthermore, I am intrigued why you didn't call DC and tell them what happened. Assaulting a Federal Officer is a federal crime. Correct?"

"Chief, I didn't call my office because I think my side had something to do with it," he said flatly.

"What?"

"The leader of the group that busted in knew my supervisor's name. He said that he told them where I was staying and what I was holding. He said they were in on it."

Marks shook his head, looking at Grey. "Holy Shit," he whispered. "Now what?"

Clark pulled the scrap of paper out of his pocket. "The leader of the group left this number. Said for me to call it and get the answers I was looking for. That's what I intend to do."

Grey thought for a moment. "How can we help, Dave?"

"Not sure yet, Chief. I'll know more after I call this number." He didn't want to say what else his attacker had said concerning *Stone Gate*. It gave him physical pain to even say the words. If all this was really connected to what happened in New Mexico, he wouldn't have to say a word; *Stone Gate* would be reaching out to him.

Chapter Twenty-Five

Briggs read the latest flash concerning the *Stone Gate* reference on his computer screen while Agent Stacy sat quietly waiting for him to finish. "All right," announced Briggs, tossing his reading glasses on the desk. "I don't think we have a choice. We're going to have to send some people out there and find out what's going on."

"I've run the entire conversation from both ends and it really sounds like there was some kind of op being run," replied Stacy. "As you can see from the transcript on your screen, there is a reference to "items" being secured and, if you scroll down, you can see that the first call that was made at the Michigan location was received by the FBI."

"Do we know where? What office?" asked Briggs, looking up, surprised.

"Ah, yes, sir, the call came out of the DC office. It's a private line. We cross checked it with the PRTN computer and found out the signal came out of the Art Crime Unit office at 19:28 hours on the twenty-third of this month - yesterday."

Briggs looked back at the screen. "Do we know the players?"

"Yes, sir. We ran the voice recognition diagnostic against the complete data file of the DC FBI employee list and got a blue line positive identifier on an Agent Rodeo Ramirez."

Briggs smiled slightly. "That's his real name? Rodeo?"

"Yes, sir. Been with the bureau for seventeen years. Clean record. Started out as a field agent. Worked his way up to team lead supervisor at the Art Crimes Unit."

"All right. Get a hold of some of our folks and have them pay Ramirez a visit. Also I'd like for you to get on a plane and find out what's going on in…. where is this town?"

"It's a town called Coloma, sir, in southwest Michigan. According to the map, about an hour from South Bend, Indiana."

Briggs sat back in his chair. "Okay, go find me some answers. If someone is playing in our back yard, I need to know about it. Also, I don't want any reference to *Operation Stone Gate* on any report or correspondence. Understand?"

"Yes, sir."

"I don't want people jumping out of windows until we find out what is going on."

"Yes, sir. I'm on it. Sir, how much of this do you want shared with the FBI?"

Briggs thought for a moment. This had always been a dicey, highly charged political position to be put in. The current administration was publically adamant about inter-governmental transparency and cooperation. But behind the curtain, where the real action takes place, things were anything but open and cooperative. The agencies who controlled the information flow, from the White House down, had put up stonewalls years ago. "Stay dark, at least until we find out what's really happening in Michigan. I don't see a need for anyone else to be involved."

"Yes, sir."

Clark had been in many morgues over the course of his career. The smell of human decay was a constant, the signature of the freshly dead hanging in the air. He needed to see the bodies of the three who committed suicide, needed to put a face on what was really happening. Deeply bothered by current events and determined to get some answers, he had had Detective Marks drive him to the Berrien County morgue.

The attendant walked over to a bank of stainless steel locker doors and checked his clipboard. "Okay, ah, your guys are in lockers six, seven, and nine." He opened locker six and slid the tray out. "Here you go. Just roll them back in when you're done."

Pulling back the sheet on the first body, Clark was struck by how physically fit the man appeared to be. Past the first stages of decomposition, he carried the muscle mass of a soldier.

"Ah, this one had the ID of Jared Gerhard Foster," announced Marks, checking the clipboard. "A German national, forty-four years old. He has an address somewhere in Milan. He's a long way from home."

"Anything on his background?" questioned Clark.

"Nothing yet. Still waiting for the Feds to get back to us. Prelim tox says cyanide killed him. Weird."

Clark leaned close, looking at a small tattoo just above the man's ankle. "See that?" he asked, lifting the man's foot.

Marks leaned close. "Looks Like a cross and a shepherd's staff. What is it?"

Clark rolled the tray back in the locker and opened number seven. This body was older and looked as if there had been very little physical activity over the course of life. "Ah, this one is a Mister Mario Amoretti, Italian national, fifty-eight years old. Has an address also in Milan. He also died by cyanide. Nothing on his background yet other than an Internet search which says he was some kind of teacher or professor in Italy."

"Check it out," replied Clark, holding up the man's foot. "Same tattoo."

"Do you know why they have them?"

Clark covered the body with the sheet and rolled the tray back in the locker. "Yeah, I do. There is a group called *The Committee* in Rome that is supposedly the keeper of very important religious artifacts, stuff that dates back to the time of Christ. We heard about them a couple of years ago but never had any need for real contact with them."

Marks opened locker nine and rolled out the tray. "This is Godolphin Abel, a forty-six-year-old Italian national. Lived in Milan. Check it out. He has the same tattoo on his ankle. What does it mean?"

Clark pushed the tray back into the locker. "That tattoo is the seal of the Vatican. It's used as an identifier of Committee members."

"So, what do we have here besides three guys who work for the Vatican committing suicide in Coloma, Michigan?" Clark pulled out his cell phone and punched in the numbers, already knowing what would be said on the other end. Seeing the dead had solidified his decision. There was no turning back. Fate, karma, or bad luck had rolled the dice again making him the loser. His attacker was right; he had no friends at the FBI. "Hey, Rodeo. I'm surprised you took my call."

"Yeah, why's that? Don't you have a plane to catch?"

Clark laughed. "C'mon, Rodeo. You're smarter than that. Your friends paid me a visit. Told me all about you setting me up. Made their job a whole lot easier."

"I have no idea what you're talking about, Dave. Look, I know you have been under a lot of stress lately. You need to catch your flight and come back to DC. We can talk about maybe some leave time then."

"You son of a bitch. So this is how you're going to play this. I'm some nut case, rogue agent who ran off the rails and made all this stuff up. Is that it?"

"Dave, where are you calling from?"

"In Michigan, where you sent me." Suddenly it all made sense - the travel office not having a record of him leaving DC, his background, now building a case about his instability. They had him by the balls, and Ramirez knew it. Anything he now said would be recorded and used against him later."

"Agent Clark, you really need to catch your flight and get ba…"

"Go fuck yourself, Rodeo," interrupted Clark. "You're not going to win this." He turned off the call and looked at Marks who didn't know what to make of what he had just heard.

"Wow, you always talk to your boss that way? Must be nice."

Clark smiled. "No, that was the first time… probably the last. I don't think I'm an FBI agent anymore."

Marks shook his head. "Judging from that, I would say you're correct. C'mon, let's get out of here. I think we have a lot to talk about."

Clark nodded. "And it's my guess we don't have a whole lot of time. This is just getting started."

Chapter Twenty-Six

De Parman had only seen the Medallions in the official photocopies that were kept in a secured vault within the Vatican library. Now, looking at the two medals on his desk just confirmed how stunningly beautiful they really are. Men had fought wars for less than this. The Bishop reached across the desk and picked up the silver Medallion.

"They really are exquisite aren't they?" he whispered, holding the medal up by the chain. The Medallions had been delivered at eight o'clock that morning and the Bishop and several other high level Vatican clergy and administrative officers had arrived at De Parman's office just five minutes later.

"Will these be stored with the rest, Your Eminence?" questioned the Chairman.

The Bishop gently laid the medal back on the desk. "For the time being. We have to prepare for the next phase of the plan."

De Parman looked at him, confused. He had assumed they were to be kept behind locked doors like most of the other religious artifacts. "The next *phase*, Your Eminence?"

The Bishop nodded for one of the administrative aids to secure De Parman's office door. "Mister Chairman, I think it's time you knew more about what having these means and what we intend to do with them."

DeParman looked around the room at the stoic faces of the entourage; whatever secret they carried did not show in their expressions. The Bishop sat back in his chair leveling a flat stare at De Parman. "You are familiar with the Book of Acts?"

"Yes, of course. The Book of Acts contains many things: the ascension of Christ, the promise of the Holy Spirit in the upper room, the apostle Paul and descriptions of his ministry."

The Bishop smiled. You know your Bible, sir. There is great wisdom in knowing the Word of God. I am pleased to see you are a student."

As in past conversations he had had with the Bishop, this one was starting the same way. He had a cryptic way of getting to his point. "We are all students when it comes to God, Your Eminence."

The Bishop drew a heavy sigh. "Maybe we are about to be more than students, Mister Chairman. For the first time in many years the thirteen sets are finally together, just as they were the day they were given to the disciples. As you recall, something world-changing happened at that time."

De Parman was stunned by the realization of what the Bishop was getting to. "Your Eminence, are you referring to the introduction of the Holy Spirit?"

The Bishop smiled. "That's exactly what we are talking about. We are going to recreate the conditions that allowed the Holy Spirit to descend from heaven. We believe that when the Medallions are together, they open a door, the door to the very gates of heaven."

De Parman shook his head confused. "But the Spirit has already descended, two thousand years ago. I don't understand?"

The Bishop reached into the pocket of his waistcoat and pulled out a cigarette and lighter. "Yes, but with the help of some of our American friends, this time we will be there to see it. It should be a very interesting thing to see. Remember, Mister Chairman, God is on our side."

****

"So, you're just going to throw away a career with the FBI, just like that?" Clark kept silent as the landscape rolled by. Marks had insisted on driving him to the airport in South Bend that afternoon, still greatly confused about all that had happened. The visit to the morgue had created more questions than answers.

"I don't have a choice, Jim. This has been coming for some time now, ever since New Mexico." His voice trailed off as a hard, vivid memory punched through. Whatever they had done to him during the reeducation confinement was still working. Even thinking about New Mexico and his involvement in the incident brought sensations of physical pain and emotional dread.

As he drove, Marks looked over. "You know, you don't have to tell me. But, is there something more to this whole case than a couple of medals that do strange things? Why have you been targeted by the FBI? It doesn't make any sense."

Clark pointed at the South Bend Airport off-ramp. "Go ahead and turn off here. I have to make a call."

Marks followed the off-ramp and pulled into the parking lot of a mini-mart as a late November rain began to fall. Clark found the piece of paper in his pocket, the note he had found in his room. He punched in the numbers. The call was answered almost immediately. "Yes."

"Who is this?" asked Clark angrily.

"This is Mister Costa. I assume this is Agent Clark of the FBI? Correct?"

"Okay, I'm Clark. Now what?"

"Very good, Agent Clark. Right to the point - classic American etiquette."

"You know, it's funny. You don't sound like a thug on the phone, Costa."

Costa chuckled. "I'm not a thug as you say, Agent Clark. I'm merely a representative of some very powerful people who would very much like to meet you."

"Meet me? About what?"

"Oh, come now, Agent Clark. Your experiences in New Mexico and the S*tone Gate* incident are very interesting to us. We would very much like to talk to you about them."

Clark thought for a moment, starting to feel the nausea rise in his stomach at the very mention of *Stone Gate*.

"I don't think I have anything to say about that, I... "

"Before you continue, Agent Clark," interrupted Costa, "I think I need to remind you of your circumstances. You see, we know that your fellow FBI comrades turned their backs on you. You are now considered to be an unbalanced employee acting in violation of direct orders. We know that those accusations are made more believable due to your history with *Stone Gate*. You have lost your wife, most if not all of your savings, and now - your job. You have nothing left but us, and we genuinely want to help."

"Helping me - by assaulting and robbing me in my hotel room, stealing evidence involved in a capital crime? Odd kind of help."

"All for the greater good, Agent Clark. And it can all be explained with your cooperation."

"What kind of cooperation?"

"Agent Clark, in six and a half hours, one of our planes will land at the South Bend, Indiana Airport. We would like you to board this plane and take a rather long journey."

"Where to?"

"To Europe."

"Don't have a passport, Costa. Besides, what makes you think I would trust you on anything? The way it sounds, I have you to blame for all of my trouble."

"Agent Clark, you do not need a passport for this flight. It is a diplomatic aircraft and you are a guest. Come now. Do you really believe you have a choice?"

"Is that a threat?"

Costa laughed. "Absolutely. This is a threat, a plea, an encouragement, anything you need it to be. Just get on the plane and start helping yourself."

Clark shook his head, feeling the box grow smaller. "I might just walk away. You ever thought about that?"

"And do what, Agent? Where will you go with no money, no references, and no friends? .....Agent Clark, are you still there? Agent Clark?"

"Yeah, I'm still here."

"As I said, the plane will be there in six hours. I hope you make the right choice. I really do."

"And if I don't show? Then what?"

The line was silent for a moment. "We all have to live with the consequences of our decisions. You will be no different. Goodbye, Agent. I wish you the best." The line went dead.

"Costa, Costa," he shouted as the rain pounded down on the windshield and roof.

"Well, what do you want to do?" questioned Marks, starting the car.

Clark slipped the phone back in his jacket, thinking. "I have to kill about six hours," he replied, shaking his head. "Let's go find someplace dry. I have a story to tell you." As they drove into the outskirts of South Bend, the rain turned into a thin sleet, coating the streets and slowing the traffic. Clark watched as the afternoon traffic slowed - commuters on their way home.

To be going home, he thought sadly. It would be wonderful. At that moment he would give anything to be in some other car, complaining about the Midwest weather, the heavy traffic, the kids, the wife, and all the rest of normal life everyone else seemed to be living. He would give anything for that, everything.

Chapter Twenty-Seven

Costa sat quietly in De Parman's office, just as he had done a thousand times before - the dutiful servant waiting for the master to finish a thought or a cup of tea. He knew it for what it was - a power play intended to remind him of who was really in charge.

"And our FBI Agent is with us?" asked the Chairman, setting his cup and saucer on the desk.

"Yes, Sir. He boarded the plane. Should be landing around nine this evening. Sir, if you don't mind my asking, why did you change your mind about eliminating him?"

De Parman smiled without humor. "He's important. He is one of the few people on this earth who has seen the continuum with his own eyes. His input into this project will be very helpful but only if he is alive."

Costa thought for a moment. For days since he had heard about the final plans, he had been struggling with deep concerns. "Sir, I hope you don't find this impertinent, but do we have the right to do what we are about to do? I mean, forgive me, but I am having a hard time believing that this is even possible, much less the vast implications if it is."

The Chairman smiled the same condescending grin. "This is going to happen, my friend, with or without your unfounded trepidation. If you have misgivings about our future plans, you would be well-served to keep them to yourself. Please notify me when the Agent arrives." He picked up the teacup, indicating the conversation was over.

Excusing himself, Costa left the room feeling a level of apprehension and dread he had not experienced in all his years of service to The Committee. This operation had changed, morphed from it's original mandate of retrieving the Medallions because of their value and power for the Church to recreating the Upper Room experience mentioned in the Book of Acts.

It was one thing to control the lives of men; it was another to tempt the hand of God. Walking back to his office, he started doing something he had not done in earnest in years - he started to pray. Deep in his heart he knew he was going to need it.

****

In all of his time dealing with air travel, Clark had never been in such an opulent jet. He was the only passenger and had been catered to by two highly efficient cabin stewards from the minute he walked in. A neatly dressed security agent had met him when he reached the top of the stairway and had asked him to give up his firearm. He had been shown his seat and served his choice of soft drink or alcohol. *So much for abstinence,* he had thought. The plush, black leather easy chair seats, the polished wood, and tan-colored interior gave the cabin a look of wealth and power. The plane was worthy of any high level diplomat or executive or, in this case, the Pope.

As he settled back into his seat, he noticed the Vatican seal embroidered into the leather headrests and on the wall plaques near the door. He recognized it as the same emblem he had seen tattooed on the ankles of the three dead men in the morgue. It was a stark reminder that this was no vacation. No matter how comfortable the surroundings, he was dealing with hard men with equally hard-edged views of control and power. They were people who would not hesitate to kill if that status was threatened. Before he boarded the plane in South Bend, he had time to tell Marks some of the story of New Mexico. He had struggled to keep his emotions in check while fighting through the painful memories. It was the first time he had ever talked about the incident, and, as expected, his story had drawn an expression of disbelief and shock from the seasoned detective.

As he told the story of those harrowing days during his first exposure to operation *Stone Gate,* he could hardly believe it himself. He had seen what only a handful of men had seen. He had seen the power of that terrible thing out there in that dusty subdivision in Albuquerque. The case had started out as a missing person's report, a random call to his office. The woman had called from Montana frantic to find her missing husband whom she had not heard from in two weeks.

The missing person was a professor at the University of Montana who had been working with a retired aeronautical engineer living in Albuquerque. He had ended up meeting the professor's wife, and together they had started a two-week odyssey in their efforts to find him. He felt the plane bank and then saw the seat belt sign blink on. Evidently they were getting close to landing.

Sitting alone in the plane, the memories of that time came back in a rush. He remembered how surreal it was to go to the husband's last known location only to find that the house had burned to the ground. The structure had not only been destroyed; the concrete foundation, the plumbing, and everything inside had been incinerated down to a fine black ash. The house's basement had been full of wispy soot. That is where he first saw the anomaly. He had been standing above, looking into the pit that was once a three-bedroom house, and even in bright sunlight, he saw the strange intensely blue light glowing from under the ash.

He had walked across the street and picked up a neighbor's shovel in order to see what and where the light was coming from. He had cautiously bent down and carefully prodded the soot when, in stunned surprise, he felt the shovel jerked from his hand, nearly pulling him in. The light did not appear to be any type of reflection. In fact he had had the impression it did not come from anything man made. It appeared to be a void in space, a gash in time, a ten-foot wide by four-foot long ragged doorway to infinity. Whatever force had blown the house to powder had torn a hole in the space-time continuum, and he had seen it with his own eyes.

Three days later, he, along with the wife of the missing professor, had been drugged, handcuffed, and basically kidnapped. Obviously, he had seen something he was not supposed to see while investigating a case that had been far too hot. For two weeks, he had been subjected to the most intense interrogation and debrief he had ever encountered, and it had all been at the hands of a shadowy government agency.

When they were finished, he was a broken man, beaten down to a shadow of his former self. He was given mandatory administrative leave and reassigned to the Art Crime Unit in Washington, a place where he could be more easily monitored and supervised. That was his encounter with *Stone Gate,* an incident that changed his life forever. They never found the woman's husband.

Feeling the plane descend, he knew he was once again under control of forces he could neither see nor fight. The fatigue he now felt behind the eyes had nothing to do with being physically tired. This was an emotional exhaustion, a weariness that settled down onto the smooth shiny rocks of his soul. He had nothing left inside. The walls were down. Even the will to see another day had faded.

The stoic security officer walked up and knelt down beside his seat. "Agent Clark, I will escort you through customs and the airport. I will hand you off to your contact inside."

"What about my weapon? When do I get it back?"

The security officer smiled. "When you're back on American soil, Agent Clark." He nodded reassuringly and then walked to the back of the plane, taking a seat near the bathroom doors.

Clark eased back in his seat, watching the green fields and then tall city buildings roll by as the plane banked hard to the left. He knew he had little to no chance of ever seeing the United States again and, at the moment, he couldn't have cared less. All they could do was kill him and, the way he felt now, it would be a blessing. He remembered the old saying - *There is nothing more dangerous than a man who has nothing to loose.* "Yeah, that fit. Goddam right," he whispered to himself.

Chapter Twenty-Eight

"Okay, where are we with this?" questioned Briggs. It had been twelve hours since he last spoke to Stacey. In Briggs' mind, there was already enough circumstantial evidence that *Stone Gate* had been compromised, enough information for direct action.

"Sir, as you know, Clark boarded the flight in South Bend for the Vatican at 18:45 last night. He should be in Rome as we speak. A second phone call was made to his contact there, a Mister Costa. I believe he is the one that Clark is meeting."

Briggs eased back in his office chair, becoming more convinced by the second of the course of action he should take. "What's going on in Michigan? How far has this spread?"

'Sir, I am currently in Coloma. It's a small town with a police force of around twenty. Clark was working with the Chief and a detective concerning some religious artifacts. Several suicides there appear to be connected to them in some way. Reports of the suicides are in all the local papers. We've already stepped on the story and kept it from being released by any of the national outlets. At this time, I have no information on how much Clark has told the detective or the Chief concerning his involvement with the New Mexico incident - if any."

Briggs thought for a moment. "All right, make contact with the Chief and the detective. Find out what his case involves and then have a come to Jesus meeting with them. Scare about three colors of shit out of them... national security, complicity after the fact, IRS trouble...you know - the normal package. Hit them hard."

"Yes, sir. And if they are uncooperative?"

"Then call the cleaning unit. You have full authority," Briggs replied without hesitation. "Let them know we are doing them a favor by talking instead of taking action. I want this shut down - now."

"Yes, sir. What did you want done with Rodriquez? We are certain that he's our leak source. From what we have gathered, he has been accessing Clark's file and selling the information. Somehow he has gotten access to the complete briefing files from Albuquerque. Our people have gone over his financials. It appears that the motive for all of his involvement is money."

For Briggs, that was all he needed to hear concerning the FBI team lead. "We'll take care of that from here. I'll order the action within the hour. Have your meeting with the locals and then stand by in Michigan. We are finalizing the last bit of this."

"Very good, sir. I will check in with you before COB today."

Briggs disconnected the call and immediately typed a message to another asset supervisor on the secure line. Within seconds, the asset responded. Briggs typed in the order:

FIRST SUBJECT :

RODEO RODRIQEZ, FBI TEAM LEADER, ART CRIMES UNIT, WASHINGTON DC. (FILE ON RECORD,) _**DIRECT ACTION, BLUE**_**...AUTHORIZED THIS DATE. ZULU, TWO SEVEN NINE SEVEN....**

SECOND SUBJECT:

AGENT DAVID CLARK, FBI, TEAM MEMBER, ART CRIMES UNIT, WASHINGTON DC, (FILE ON RECORD,) *DIRECT ACTION*, *BLUE*...AUTHORIZED THIS DATE, ZULU, TWO SEVEN NINE EIGHT...ALL REFERANCES TO ACTION FALL UNDER THE PERAMETERS OF STONE GATE. TS /SCI READ IN. AUTHORIZING OFFICER /// E , J BRIGGS. LEVEL / YANKEE / WHITE.... end of message.

That was all it took to change a life or take the life of someone he had never met, nor would have ever met. There are some secrets that cannot be shared as the consequences are severe for doing so. In Briggs' mind, divulging highly classified national security information for profit was the lowest of the low as far as criminality was concerned. *Stone Gate* information would be protected at all cost. The Art Crimes Team leader had sealed his and Agent Clark's fate the second that he had put a price on that information.

Briggs had been surprised at how sloppily Rodriquez had run his operation. Was he really so naive to believe that his "secure" lines of communication were not being monitored? Did he honestly think he could say the words "Stone Gate" and not be flagged for investigation? The level of the man's stupidity was amazing. In his mind, someone that dumb, especially while carrying an FBI credential, should not even be alive.

****

Four thousand miles east of Briggs' office, Clark was moving through the brightly lit streets of the Tavares Piazza roundabout on his way to the Vatican. He watched out the van window as it crossed the Tiber River on the bridge, the Pons Sublicisus, an ornate, highly used span that had been reconstructed after WWII, and he was struck by how beautiful the city looked in the dark. The orange, muted glow of a thousand mercury vapor streetlights gave the entire area a gauzy, dream-like glow. In the distance, the brightly lit red walls of Vatican City rose out of the darkness, magnificent, yet oddly foreboding.

At any other time, he would have been in awe, seeing the Eternal city lit up in all it's romantic glory, but tonight, as he rode quietly in the back of the van, he felt nothing but dread. For the hundredth time since he had landed, he took a mental stock of his situation, the deep recesses of his survival instinct running fifty different scenarios at a time. What would he say? How would he say it? More importantly, how would anything he had to offer save his life? He was in a foreign country with no money, no passport, and no tangible authorization for even being there.

Approaching the expansive arch, the driver dimmed his headlights and slowed. A uniformed gate guard quickly waved them through. Clark watched as the van headlights swept across the expansive grounds and neatly manicured shrubbery that lined the road. Minutes later they turned into a well lit, wide, smooth concrete parking lot in front of a multi-story palace. The opulence was incredible. As he stepped from the van, he was immediately met by a short, well-dressed man in a dark suit and several uniformed police officers in full tactical gear.

"Agent Clark," announced the man stepping forward, extending his hand. "I am Mister Costa. We talked on the phone." Clark shook his hand, trying to fight through the surreal fog of the moment. He was being greeted as a friendly guest, something he had not expected. Costa motioned towards the front door of the palace. "I trust your trip was not too bad?" he said cheerfully. "The Chairman is in his office. I assume you would want to have some of your questions answered right away, if you're not too tired that is."

As he followed the aid up the stairs, Clark was startled to hear a familiar voice behind him. "Glad you made it, Agent. I hope there are no hard feelings?" Clark quickly turned around as one of the tactically dressed officers stepped forward, removing his helmet and balaclava as his submachine gun hung to the side. Stunned, Clark immediately recognized the red hair. The man smiled, "I think we've met before. I'm Simms. Welcome to the Vatican."

Chapter Twenty-Nine

Emil Delany and his two-man team of engineers had been working on the drone for a month now and were fairly certain that when the command to use it came across the wire, it would perform the mission as required. They had been meticulous in the installation of the Iranian munitions and computer hardware, right down to the server-board numerical designations, equipment that could only come from the Republican guard munitions depot and their Ministry of Defense.

The after-action forensic team down range would pour over the remaining explosive debris after the attack and would determine that the bomb had been built by Iranian agents. Of course that would be the wrong assumption but, when faced with the physical evidence, no other assumption would hold water. The Raad 85, or suicide drone as it was called, had been stolen by Free Force operatives from a munitions supply cache just after the fall of the Kaddafi Government in Libya in 2012. The drone, along with tons of other munitions, from AK 47s to RPGs, had been driven away by the truck load and had been responsible for much of the death and dismemberment in the ongoing Libyan civil war ever since.

Emil picked up the secure line sat-phone on the second ring. "Yes, I'm here." He sat back in his desk chair, trying to relieve the tightness in his back. He hadn't left the office in days; getting the last of the telemetry programming together had been a tedious, meticulous endeavor with zero room for error. A distant burp of heavy automatic weapons' fire echoed through the warm night as the familiar voice of his supervisor and point of contact came on the line. "Is the package ready for delivery?"

Emil lit one of the Libyan cigarettes from the pack, a super strong, non-filtered nail of lung destruction. "Yes, it's ready. What's the time frame?" More gunfire could be heard, this time further away - a nightly affair in present day Tripoli.

"We are on a forty-eight hour window. Are you sure the package can be delivered? It's imperative."

Emil, in all of his thirty plus years of working for the Agency, hated this question, this seemingly innocuous inquiry, the most. It always came down to an absolute - his word and his guarantee that the mission would be successful. They always wanted someone's name on the blame line. Of course he could not guarantee that the drone with its twenty-five kilo payload of Iranian high explosives would hit the target. A million things could go wrong. The wind could shift. The server communication could break down. There could be detonation failure. Human error could blow the whole thing up before it even left the sled, killing him and everyone else within fifty meters. Any of it could happen before the bomb ever hit the target.

"Yes, the package will be delivered," he replied, blowing a lungful of smoke to the ceiling. Imperative? Shit, in this country everything he did was imperative.

"Excellent. As I said, we have a forty-eight hour window but my guess is that the delivery will happen within the next twelve to fifteen hours. I will contact you the minute I get the word. Please be ready."

Emil snuffed out the smoke. *God these are awful,* he thought. "I will be standing by," he replied. He ended the call and tossed the phone on the desk, trying to remember when he ate last. Strangely enough there was a pretty good Chinese take-out just down the street, and at the moment that seemed to be what sounded good. He had been stationed in Libya for over a year now and had been able to move in and out of this shadowy world with relative ease. The country was crawling with spooks, the crazy-brave, and enough religious zealots to fill two stadiums.

The grease that turned all the wheels of the death machine in present-day Libya was money and everybody wanted it. He stayed alive by paying the people who wanted to kill him, the closet queers with guns and the blood-in-the-eye killers who got off on it all. There was never an overt threat from his protectors, but sideways glances and the low whispers let him know he was only a failed payday away from a bullet through the eye and a third-world landfill grave.

Americans had worn out their welcome in the Middle East years ago and were now only tolerated for the cash they could produce. All the heavy hitters and Jihad shot-callers from Afghanistan to Nigeria had long since lost their fear of the American war machine and all the crippled wolves that ran it. The United States President was considered a nut-less stooge by the rest of the world and totally inept at addressing the growing threat and power of extremism now sweeping the world. The meat-eaters were out of the cage, and nothing the Americans said or did was going to put them back in it.

No, this kind of operation was old school, put in motion by men who still drank Scotch whisky before five and told their wives only what they needed to know. They did not *share* their day; the action was far too heavy for conversation over pot roast. This mission was how things used to be done. Bad guys, who had been deemed a threat, were going to die, and the blame would fall hot and wet right at the feet of people who deserved just as much heat. Emil looked over at the large, sand-colored drone that sat in the middle of the shop floor, shining under the florescent lights and smiled. *Yeah, old school*, he thought, snapping off the lights. *Gonna be fun.*

***

Six hours behind and a world away, Briggs stepped out of a black government limousine in front of the Prime Rib Steakhouse on K street in downtown DC, an old guard haunt where half the Washington deals went down as smooth as the bourbon. Without stopping at the maître dé station, he walked to the back tables. To the wait-staff, the three men at the table carried the same air of power and privilege as a lot of other government elites that floated in an out of the place. Senior members of Congress, military heavy hitters, and powerful lobbyist were all members of the club. They were eager participants in a game where the really dangerous men wore three thousand dollar suits and traded political firepower just as fast and deadly as they could throw it.

Briggs pulled up his customary chair as the other three sat quietly sipping their drinks. "So, how are things progressing? All is in order, I trust?" The question had come from Neil Holloway, the National Security Liaison Director, a retired Army-05 deep into the DC culture of power and influence with little patience for small talk.

Briggs nodded to the waiter who brought his martini before answering. "Everything is on track," he replied after taking a sip. "Assets are in place. Should have all the pieces in play within twelve hours."

Holloway leaned forward, resting his elbows on the table. "You still think the fallout is manageable on this?" he asked, leveling a steady gaze at Briggs. "The consequences could be severe."

Briggs thought for a moment. "Considering what's at stake, I would say the fall out, if any, is very manageable. The outrage that will be felt worldwide after this will not be directed at us but at the Iranians and wild-eyed Jihadists. To me, it's a win on both fronts."

Jake Montrose, the youngest of the group, spoke up. "What's the plan for dealing with our leak downtown?" Despite his relatively young age of thirty-eight, he was considered an operational genius within the narrow walls of the intelligence community. Having made a stellar reputation as a member of DEVGRP, better known as SEAL Team-Six in Iraq and Afghanistan and being an honor graduate from Norte Dame, had pushed him into the rarefied air of beyond *Top Secret* Intelligence operations. He was currently the CIA's section leader for Special Projects in DC, a role that the other men at the table knew was only a stepping stone to bigger and better things.

Briggs took another sip of his drink before answering. He respected Montrose but there was something in his personality Briggs just didn't care for. Maybe it was the abrasive, over-the-top self-assuredness the ex-SEAL exhibited or the way Montrose could look you in the eye with that smirk that just seemed to say *fuck you*. Briggs set his glass back on the table, looking around the room. The early evening dinner crowd was just starting to filter in. "It's being taken care of as we speak."

The fourth man at the table had remained quiet, slowly nursing the bourbon he always had with his steak. Of the four, he carried the most power and influence of any of the others. He was Mason Braid, the Deputy Director of an agency informally known as the *Kingdom,* a dark-as-coal organization that had its roots firmly seated in the original Majestic Twelve days of the Truman Administration. The Kingdom ran the *Stone Gate* mission and several other operations that only a handful of men in The United States had been read into. Not even the President of the United States had access to the mission papers and back briefs of the Kingdom. "I would like this to go forward before the close of business tomorrow," he announced softly.

"Sir," replied Briggs, "I'm not sure things will be ready by then. We are still gathering information on the target package."

"JP, every minute that goes by puts everything we have worked for in jeopardy. I am well aware of the operational redundancy your team likes to have before action is taken, and I appreciate your efforts, but my time-line for action is not a request. I want the slate wiped clean - immediately." Braid scanned the faces of the other men. "Is there any confusion concerning my wishes?"

Briggs shook his head. "No, sir," he replied, answering for the others. Braid smiled without humor before downing the last of his whiskey. "All right, JP, from what you have gathered, do you really think these people can accomplish what they have planned?"

"We are not sure what will happen. Several of our experts have said that it's all a bunch of religious clap-trap. Others have said that the medals are real and that getting them all in the same room could make something extraordinary happen."

"And, what do you think, JP? What's your opinion of the Medallions and their power?"

Briggs thought for a moment. "Sir, I don't believe in Bigfoot, the Easter Bunny, or Santa Claus. Nor do I believe in a piece of metal that gives a person the ability to fly or be invisible. I also agree that every minute that information about our endeavors is floating around is a minute that unnecessarily puts everything at risk."

Braid motioned for the waiter to bring the check. "Very well, then we have nothing else to discuss. I will expect the after-action report on my desk by tomorrow afternoon. Gentlemen, if you will excuse me, I have another engagement." Briggs shook hands with Braid as he left the table, sealing his fate to whatever would or would not happen three thousand miles away within the next twelve hours. A lot was riding on the stubby carbon-fiber wings of the device now quietly sitting in the dark a continent away. If successful, the event would start a religious war unparalleled since the crusades. An attack on the Vatican would cause such blind rage within the world community, that in it's blood lust for revenge, any gains made within the Muslim extremist movement would be wiped out overnight.

For Briggs, he really could not see a downside. If it worked, he would have killed several birds with one stone. If it did not, it would not matter. His life would be over within hours. In his mind, as a true believer, it was all within the parameters of acceptable risk, a code he had lived by his entire life in service to the greater good. It was the price you had to pay to be in the club, a price way too high for most men. Other people's blood always came with a price…always.

Chapter Thirty

Rodeo never liked carrying his FBI-issued weapon. He found it uncomfortable and cumbersome on the beltline. Because he spent most of his working hours at a desk, the Sig Saur 9mm stayed in his drawer, only seeing the light of day twice yearly during range-qualifications. Not that the weapon would save him that evening, even if he did have it with him. The agent would become a victim of his habits, his routine - easy to track, easy to follow. He always stopped at the Red Spot Diner on Washington Avenue after leaving work. The waitress there was a pretty twenty-eight-year-old brunette that he had been trying to go out with for several weeks now. Since his divorce last year, he had been hitting on just about every woman he took a liking to, a character flaw that had already cost him two marriages. For all his education and career advancement, Rodeo Rodriquez was a womanizer, someone incapable of faithfulness and fidelity. He just could not help himself.

****

"What time is it now?" The man sitting in the passenger side of the car checked his watch. They had been sitting in their car across the street from the diner since four-thirty, waiting for their target.

"Ah, it's about ten after six. He should be showing up any time now," he replied, adjusting his back in the seat. "Let's make this as quick as we can. My kid has a game tonight."

The driver smiled. "How old is she now - ten, eleven?"

The passenger laughed. "I wish. Just turned thirteen, a teenager now."

"Wow, they grow up fast. What's it like having all that estrogen in the house, anyway?"

"It's brutal, pard. You would not believe what I spend on paper products. Having two grown females in the house is a freak'in battlefield."

The driver nodded. "There's our guy. He just pulled up in that black Range Rover."

The passenger pulled the radio from his coat pocket. "All units, package has arrived. Repeat. Package has arrived. We have a thirty to forty minute window. Stand by."

"You know, anybody who drives that kind of four wheel drive vehicle in the city and never gets off the road has got to be a dick."

The passenger laughed. "No shit. I hate guys like that. So, how you want to do this? We have some latitude."

The driver drank down the last of his Red Bull and tossed the can into the back seat. "Well, let's just take him like the last guy. Take him out in his car when he comes back out. It's quiet and quick. You want me to badge him?"

"Naw, I'll take him," replied the passenger, pulling the pistol from the gun box on the floor. The weapon had been his choice in close quarter battle for years: a Ruger, Mark 3.22 long rifle pistol, the barrel threaded an inch and a half from the tip, accepting a black steel Gentec suppressor. The subsonic ammunition coupled with the suppressor would make the hit nearly silent.

Twenty minutes later, the men watched as Rodriquez stepped out of the restaurant and onto the sidewalk, clearly illuminated by the streetlights and the overhead sign. Without a word, the men stepped out of the car and quickly walked across the busy street. Less than thirty feet away from the back of Rodeo's car, they waited for him to unlock his door. Seconds after he slid in behind the wheel of the Range Rover, the man knocked on the driver's side window.

Initially startled by the sudden appearance of a man at his window, Rodeo just as quickly relaxed seeing the DC Police uniform and badge under the man's open black rain coat. He rolled down the window. "Something I can help you with, officer?" He asked, smiling. "I didn't park in a red zone, did I?"

The man suddenly brought the pistol up and fired. Phat, phat, phat, three quick rounds into Rodeo's left eye and he was dead before he even knew he'd been shot. The shooter calmly leaned in through the window of the Range Rover, sticking the barrel into Rodeo's left ear and fired again, phat! In less than a minute it was done and the men had melted into the late evening Washington commuter traffic. Another loose end had been taken care of - a murder most perfect.

***

Clark checked his watch trying to count the hours since he had slept last. They had shown him to a small ornately decorated office located up a flight of stairs and down a long hallway. Costa had offered coffee, obviously trying to be as congenial as he could under the circumstances.

"You want to tell me what I'm doing here?" Clark asked, setting the cup and saucer on the edge of the expansive desk. They appeared to be waiting for someone as Costa had obviously been doing his best to fill the time with small talk. It was chitchat that Clark had been growing increasingly impatient with.

"I think it's best that the Chairman be here to answer your questions," replied Costa. "He should be here anytime now."

Before Clark could reply, De Parman opened the door to the office and stepped inside. "Agent Clark, it's a pleasure to meet you," he announced extending his hand. Sorry to have kept you waiting. I'm sure you're tired after the flight. Would you like some coffee, maybe something to eat?"

"No, thanks. Listen, guys, we need to cut the bullshit and get to telling me why I am here. I don't want coffee or food or anything else. What I want - are some answers."

"Easy, mate," mumbled Simms who had been standing quietly in the back of the room.

Clark turned in his chair. "Hey, dude, go fuck yourself. You and I have some unfinished business."

Simms smiled, stepping forward. "I'll save a spot for you on my dance card, tough guy. Any time any…"

"That's enough!" announced Costa, looking at Simms. "We are going to control the hostilities. Is that clear?"

Simms nodded and stepped back. "It's clear."

Clark turned back to De Parman. "All right, you got me here. Now what do you want?"

The Chairman flashed a condescending grin. "Information, Agent Clark, very important information. We know that you have been involved with the Stone Gate Operation. That is something that is of great interest to us."

"Why?"

"Agent Clark, you know precisely why. You have seen the anomaly. You have looked into the abyss of infinite time. Only a handful of men since the beginning of time have done that."

"I think you have over estimated my informational contribution to whatever you're trying to do here," replied Clark. "And, as a matter of fact, I still don't have a clear idea of what I saw that day. What I do know is that whatever it was, it ruined my career and landed me in a Government run debrief and re-educational facility that damn near killed me. Past that I don't know anything."

De Parman thought for a moment, easing his great bulk into the plush red leather office chair. "Agent Clark, do you know what we are trying to do here?"

"Don't care."

"De Parman smiled. "Oh, I think you care deeply. Your classic American tough-guy indifference is not hiding how you truly feel."

"Is that right?"

"Yes, that's right, Agent Clark. You would not have gotten on the plane and come here if you did not have the keenest of interest in our endeavors."

"Let me tell you what, pard, I am an American Federal agent, dully sworn to enforce the laws of the United States and that includes murder, kidnapping by coercion, and theft of private property, all crimes you people are up to your pious necks in. Now, whatever you plan to do with me, let's get on with it. I'm tired of being jerked around."

De Parman leaned close. "Agent Clark, I really don't think you realize the incredible opportunity you have before you. The Medallions are a gateway to God. The information you process could help us understand the spiritual realm even more."

Clark shook his head. "You people are insane. The Gateway operation, if it even exists, is a highly classified Government project that I have nothing, and I repeat, nothing to do with. I don't know why you're not getting that. I agree the medals appear to be incredible and have astonishing power but other than me being assigned to go get them…" He stopped talking, suddenly realizing that his entire connection with the Medallions had been planned. The whole thing was a set up to get him into this office. "This has all been arranged," he said quietly.

De Parman smiled. "Yes it has. Because of your connection with the anomaly, as brief as it was, your presence is needed here, needed for the next phase of this project. We have been working with our people in the discovery of the secret of *Stone Gate* ever since Dr. Taylor first found a way to access the continuum. The search for the Medallions has been ongoing since they were lost just after the war. Don't you see, Agent Clark, that you are part of a grand plan?"

"And what grand plan would that be?"

De Parman eased back in his chair, all expression leaving his face. For a moment, Clark thought the man was about to cry. "To touch the face of God, Agent Clark," he whispered. "To touch the face of God."

Chapter Thirty-One

By six-thirty the next morning, Delany was already at the docks literally waiting for his ship to come in. The lethal cargo had been loaded on the truck by five and driven from the warehouse to the docks of the Benghazi port just a short distance away. Looking out into the harbor, Delany wiped the sweat away from his face and neck. It was already ninety degrees outside but the perspiration coming off his brow was from something other than the merciless Libyan sun. He could not remember a mission or operation where the stakes were higher. By tomorrow, the world would have changed, and he was one of the main players involved in that change.

For the hundredth time since arising in the predawn darkness, he went over all the variables of the mission. From Libya to the high walls of the Vatican, the distance was exactly six hundred and thirty-two miles, a far greater range than the drone could achieve. Because of that, the mission called for the aircraft to be launched from a ship within less than half that distance. From that range, the latest in hydrogen fuel cells installed in the aircraft would be more than ample to deliver the cargo of high yield explosives.

A shipboard launch had several things in its favor that made it ideal. First, the craft could be prepped on deck more easily than in a land based setting, a location that always carried the risk of casual observation. Secondly, the ship itself could be scuttled into deep water directly after the launch, removing the launch platform and the exact location from further investigation. And third, a seaborne launch of a destructive device against a fixed facility had never been done before, and it's probability for success would be considered low. That assumption made it much more favorable as far as Delany was concerned. At seventy miles off the Italian Coast, Delany's tech should be able to hit an eight by eight foot target without even trying. With laser guided telemetry and satellite GPS coordination, navigation to the intended target would be assured. A Delay Detonation Transmitter or DDT had been engineered into the drone, a device first invented prior to the last Israeli/Arab conflict by the IDF for bunker busting. The transmitter delayed detonation upon impact a full second and a half, allowing the missile or delivery system time for deeper penetration into the target. If properly employed, the damage to the building and its occupants would be devastating.

From any casual observer, the hundred and twenty foot white and green fishing troller, *Marie De Angelo,* looked like a thousand other boats and ships that sailed over the deep blue waters off the Italian coast. Aside from the large fishing net booms on each side of the ship, the only thing different about the vessel was the large tarpaulin-covered structure close to the bow.

Up on deck, Delany turned on his laptop and ran a second diagnostic check of the drone's navigation and weapon's system. Confident that all was in order, he then downloaded the SATCOM FIVE uplink, establishing a comms recognition signature between all three operating systems. Once the bird left the deck, it would fly and hit it's intended target while under military satellite control. Finding that the system links were sound, he closed down his computer and smiled, confident that he had prepared the craft to the best of his ability. He would not say a prayer for whoever was going to be on the receiving end of the drone. In his mind, they didn't have one.

****

That same morning, six hundred miles to the east, Clark was sipping his coffee in the small dining room just down the hall from the room he had slept in the night before. Costa had arrived at seven, eager to talk.

"I trust you got some rest?" he asked, taking a seat at Clark's table. They were the only two in the room. The smell of baking bread wafted in the air from the small kitchen behind a set of tall, red wooden doors.

"What's my status here?" asked Clark with a sigh. "I don't think your boss believed me when I said I didn't have much information about *Stone Gate*." Every time he said the words, a small ball of fear and discomfort rolled in his stomach. Whatever mental conditioning they had done during his re-education confinement a year and a half ago was still working.

"You are a guest, a very important guest. Hopefully you are starting to see how much of a role you could have in what we are trying to do."

Clark shook his head. "I'll tell you what I see. For all the spiritual insight this place is supposed to possess, I think you guys are really playing with fire. No pun intended. And as far as trying to somehow connect it to the *Stone Gate* operation - that's just suicide."

"So, you are saying *Stone Gate* is real?"

"What I'm saying is that I think you're out of your depth. The power and capabilities of the Medallions is real. I've seen it with my own eyes. Haven't you guys ever thought that maybe the medals have been separated all these years for a reason?"

"And in your mind, what reason would that be?"

"I don't know - divine intervention, some kind of spiritual law we don't know about," he said, amazed that Costa seemed blind to any argument as to why the Medallions had been apart for so long. "I'm still foggy on what you people are trying to accomplish with this move."

Costa thought for a moment before answering. It was a question that hung in the air like a bad smell. "All men yearn to make sense of their existence, to know why they are alive and, in a deeper sense, to draw closer to the Creator. Honestly, I really don't know what will happen when the Medallions are put together. None of us do. But if there is a chance to gain a deeper insight to God, no matter how slight, I am willing to take that chance."

Clark smiled. "What if God isn't interested in your quest for deeper insight? What if you end up pissing Him off by pounding on His door? A lot of bad things happen when God gets upset. I'm sure there is a Bible around here somewhere. You guys ought to read it."

Costa sipped the last of his coffee. "God is merciful," he replied softly. "He has always rewarded those who seek wisdom."

Clark could see that Costa really believed in what he was doing. Being in the presence of a true believer drew a myriad of emotions running the scale from admiration for the loyalty to the cause to melancholy because of the toll and sacrifice it took for such faith - faith in something you could not see, hear, or touch. Amazing.

****

It was a little after eight when Marks pulled into the parking lot behind the PD. He still had not heard from Clark and was more than a little concerned about his welfare. He had been up all night, unable to sleep, trying to figure out his next move. The Chief had advised him to close out the Robashaw investigation and generally let things settle down. Getting out of his car, he noticed the dark sedan parked two slots over from his unit. It was strange to see the unknown civilian vehicle parked in a lot specifically designated for police cars. He walked over for a closer look and discovered the rental car sticker on the side window.

"That's mine. I'll move it."

Marks turned to the voice behind him. A tall, well-dressed man in his mid forties was quickly heading in his direction. "Yeah, this is only police parking. You can park in front of the building. That lot is always open."

The man stepped up close - uncomfortably close and smiled. "Tell you what, Detective Marks. I'll park this car wherever I feel like parking it."

Marks was suddenly caught off guard by the man's instantly threatening demeanor. "Who the hell are you, pal, and how do you know my name?" he asked, reaching for his weapon.

The man held up an official government credential. "National Security Agency, Detective. You and I need to talk. Have a seat in my car."

Marks stood dumbfounded, still not sure what was happening. He looked across the lot and saw Chief Grey standing by the back door, looking as if he had just had his nuts ripped off. He sadly nodded to Marks and then disappeared back into the building.

"I asked nice, Officer Marks. I won't be so nice if I have to say it again," Stacy announced, opening the passenger side door. "Get in the god-dammed car."

Riding through downtown in silence, Marks hadn't felt this kind of oppressive tension since he was a kid. Fighting for an emotional ledge to stand on, he grew angry. "Hey listen, I'm going to need to see that credential of yours. Knock off the tough guy bullshit. I'm a sworn police officer in this state and…"

"That's enough," interrupted Stacy, pulling the car into the nearly vacant post office parking lot. "I know who you are, Detective. In fact, I know just about everything there is to know about you and your life. You're a small town cop, in a backwater town that no one ever hears about. You make less than thirty-five thousand dollars a year. You're up to your neck in debt and owe three thousand dollars in back taxes that you're trying to pay off with monthly payments. How am I doing so far, Detective?"

"I, ah, how do,,?"

"How do I know all this about you? Is that what you're trying to say?"

"Yes."

"I know this information because I have the power and the ability to learn everything I need to know about you. I also have the ability to use that information any way I see fit. You still want to see my credential? …..Good boy," announced Stacy putting the car in park and turning off the ignition. "Sit there. Keep your mouth shut and listen to what I am about to tell you and you may just keep yourself out of a federal prison or worse."

"What's worse than federal prison?"

Stacy leveled an icy stare. "You really want to push this, Marks, because if you do, this conversation can go in a whole new direction. I'm here to do you a favor, Detective. So what's it going to be?"

"Okay, I'm listening."

Stacy held the gaze a moment longer and then reached into his suit jacket pocket, pulling out a sheet of paper. "Sign it."

"What is this?" asked Marks, taking the sheet.

"It's a secrecy oath affidavit. It relates to a highly classified government project."

"You're telling me the Medallions are a government secret?"

Stacy shook his head. "Not the Medallions, Marks, *Stone Gate*, and if you tell me you don't know what I am talking about, I'm going to put your head through that windshield."

Marks could not escape the surrealism of the moment. He could not remember the last time he had been physically threatened by anyone, much less by someone of authority. Looking into the hard eyes of the man, he decided to not push the issue. He unfolded the sheet and scribbled his name on the line at the bottom. He now understood the fear he had seen in Clark's face when the words *Stone Gate* had been mentioned.

Stacy took the paper back, his demeanor still hostile. "All right, here is what you're going to do from this moment on. You're going to forget about *Stone Gate*. You will not write anything about it or discuss it. If we find out you have, Detective Marks, and you can be rest assured we will be monitoring your activity for the foreseeable future, the full weight of the United States Government will descend upon you and your family….. Do you love your mother?"

"What kind of question is that?"

"A non rhetorical one, Detective. Answer the god-dammed question."

"Of course I love her. What does she have to do with this?"

"Nothing really, Detective. But if you break our little agreement, I will make sure her social security payments are delayed, let's say, about a year pending a review. I will also make sure she has a real close audit from the IRS every year to look forward to."

Marks shook his head in disbelief. "You would do that to someone?"

Stacy started the car. "Faster then you can imagine, Detective. So do I have your attention?"

Marks thought for a moment. "Just what exactly is *Project Stone Gate?*"

Marks watched the color drain from the man's face. "It's something that does not exist, Detective, and if you say those words again, our deal is off and your life suddenly turns into a mountain-high pile of shit. Are we clear?"

Marks could see the stretched thread now holding his life together. "We're clear. Not a problem," he replied softly.

Stacy nodded. "We are not kidding around, Detective. You screw this up, and I won't have to kill you. You'll eat your own gun after we are done with you."

"I said there won't be a problem. I got the message."

Stacy dropped the car in gear and slowly eased out of the parking lot. "Very good, Detective. Your Chief said the same thing. Maybe there is an island of intelligence in this part of Michigan. Stay in your box, Marks. You'll live longer."

Chapter Thirty-Two

According to Costa, the ceremony duplicating the event recounted in the Book of Acts would take place at seven o'clock that evening. No expense or detail had been spared in the duplication of the Upper Room described in the Bible. Stone masonry of the area and likeness of the time had been brought to the Congrieto main floor reception room, turning the Grand Hall with its priceless frescos, tapestries, and Rodin bronzes into a small cave, dimly lit by oil lamps and candles. Valuable Frankincense now burned in golden cantors throughout the room, filling the hall with a gauzy haze and for Clark the familiar aroma of a Roman Catholic funeral.

The structure of the natural stone from the Middle East stood in the center of the high ceiling ballroom looking very much like a large sand-colored igloo. As Clark sat near the back of the hall watching the preparations for the ceremony, he was struck by how the Church's representatives had been treating him with a casual friendliness. As congenial as they had been, he was under no illusion that he was not a prisoner and that his fate was still very much in question. Even though he had been given free access to the building, he was "advised" that he should not go outside as this might... *"be of some concern."*

As workmen continued to set up the room with oil lamps, stones, and period piece carpets, Costa walked in carrying what looked like a large bundle of choir robes in his arms. He sat down next to Clark with a sigh. "Incredible isn't it?" he said looking at the large rock structure sitting in the middle of the room.

"You really think you guys are going to be able to call down the fire from heaven? It is pretty risky if you ask me."

Costa smiled. "You think it's the height of arrogance to try?"

Clark thought a moment, not sure of what kind of answer Costa was fishing for. "Arrogance maybe, but I know that I read somewhere in the Bible that you're not supposed to tempt God. I'm thinking your event here fits the very definition of that."

Costa handed him one of the purple and white robes. "One size fits all. You are invited to the ceremony. The gallery will be sitting over there. The Bishop and the Cardinals will be inside the structure conducting the Mass."

Clark shook his head. "Thanks for the invitation, but this room is the last place I want to be. If you folks actually bring something down from heaven…well, on my best day I don't think God is a fan of mine."

Costa smiled. "You really believe that?"

"Until I see something different, that's my impression," replied Clark, handing the robe back.

"I guess each man has to find his own way to God."

Clark stood up. "Hey look, I have to get some air. As good as that stuff smells, it's getting pretty smoky in here. Since we're talking like old friends, why don't you tell me what happens to me. When is the honeymoon over?"

Costa stood up, picking up the bundle of robes. "The Committee Intelligence unit leader and his team will begin talking to you tomorrow."

"You mean 'interrogating' me?"

Costa would not look him in the eye as he started to walk away. "In case you change your mind," he replied, handing Clark one of the robes.

"You do mean 'interrogated', right?" called Clark, watching Costa leave the room, the sound of his voice echoed throughout the hall. He knew at that moment that everything he understood about *Stone Gate*, along with any subconscious connection he had with the anomaly, would soon be in the hands of his keepers. As he walked out of the hall, the spiritual ambiance of his surroundings began to sink in. He was wandering the halls of the Vatican, the center of spiritual reality for millions of people around the world.

Walking on the smooth white marble floor, he could almost feel the weight of all the prayers and hope that seemed to hang heavy in the natural air. He stopped on the landing of the stairs leading toward his room to study a large painting of Saint Francis of Assisi. A Master painter had captured a hint of radiant sunlight behind the bigger than life subject, giving it an ethereal glow that radiated from the confines of an ornate golden frame.

Clark studied the eyes in the painting, looking for a truth, a message... a direction. Over the years he had done this before, put himself in the presence of religious imagery while quietly asking God for help, for money, or for wisdom. When his father had died unexpectedly, he was only seventeen. He remembered walking home from school a week after the funeral and, for reasons he still did not understand, had quietly walked into the large white Methodist church that stood two blocks from his house.

He had never been in the building before, yet once inside he felt comfortable, peaceful in the hushed atmosphere of the sanctuary. Colored muted sunlight from the stained glass windows had cast a soothing glow over the padded pews and floor as he had slowly walked down the aisle to sit in the front row. A large natural wooden cross hung high above and behind the pulpit completing the picture in his mind of what a meeting place for God and all his angels should be. Church had not been a family priority, but on that day, at that moment, sitting alone in a church he had never stepped foot in before, he wanted it...no, needed it...to be the most important thing in his life. His father had been his hero, a man he loved and admired, a father who went the extra mile whenever he had the means and opportunity. And at that moment, he needed to know why God had taken him away. He remembered crying out for an answer about why his father had died. He had waited for a response that never came. With tears filling his eyes, he asked again and again only to be met by silence.

Since that day, he had carried a quiet grudge against God, a deep-seated distrust of the church and all those who stood behind the pulpit proclaiming to have the answers. In his nearly fifty years on the planet, none of them, or God for that matter, had given him the reason his father had dropped dead that warm July afternoon while working on his lawn mower...no one. Years later, he had obtained a copy of the medical examiners report of his father's autopsy. The cause of death had been marked "undetermined." He had just died and that was it. There had been a total system shut down for no apparent reason.

As he looked up at the painting, he realized he had never felt more alone. The painting had given him the same message he had received in that quiet empty church a lifetime ago. The silence seemed to mock his inability to connect. Maybe God had more important things to do than to listen to him. Cold comfort indeed.

Chapter Thirty-Three

In his office downstairs, in the non-descript glass and steel building just off the 495 Freeway near Alexandria, Mason Braid picked up the government secure phone on the second ring. "Yes."

"Sir, Briggs here. Wanted to give you an update on our project."

"Okay, go ahead."

"The players are all in place. We can initiate within the next two hours. We've contacted our folks in the press, and they will be running the story that an Iranian faction was responsible for the incident."

"All right. As it stands now, do we have any casualty projections?"

"No, sir. We do not have that number and probably won't until an after action report and general BDA is conducted."

Braid thought for moment. "Okay, green light this as soon as you're ready. Pull the trigger. A message needs to be sent. They were warned a year ago that their research and their attempts to gain access to our people would not be tolerated."

"Sir, you do know that the FBI agent involved in the *Stone Gate* project is still in the facility?

"I'm aware of that. I also know that he went there voluntarily. For that, he is responsible. Thank you for the information. Notify me when you are at a five minute window."

"Yes, sir."

Braid ended the call, still not convinced that the current operation would fully get the message across. He, along with a small group of scientists and quantum physics engineers, had been working nearly non-stop for almost two years, perfecting *the Process*. Tremendous gains had been made since Dr. Taylor's discovery had come to light. *Stone Gate* was now an integral part of the United States intelligence apparatus and had to be protected at all cost.

As he told Briggs, a message was going to be sent, a sharp edged lesson for those who might even attempt to steal or subvert any facet of *Stone Gate*. There would be no quarter, no negotiations. The only consideration they would receive after the incident would be a phone call, a single message, letting any survivors know that their plans had been discovered, and if they did not stop their project, severe and selective punishment would continue.

He was aware of the Committee's plan to perform some kind of religious Mass involving the Cabbalist Medallions, mindless nonsense as far as he was concerned. It had become just an ironic bit of luck that the members of the Italian project would all be in one place at the same time.

Braid was always amazed when government organizations like the Vatican did not have better counter surveillance equipment and cyber protection procedures in place. Every phone call, every Internet inquiry and internal communication message had been monitored and logged for years. An organization such as the Catholic Church that influenced the lives of tens of millions had to be watched.

****

Deep in the bottom of the Marie De Angelo, Delany crawled on his hands and knees below the boiler deck just off the top of the bilges peeling off the adhesive strips on the C-4 blocks and sticking them to the steel hull. He then double primed the blocks with blasting caps, stringing all ten charges together with waterproof Det Cord and electrical tape. The explosives ran almost the entire length of the hull and, when detonated, would send the ship to the bottom in seconds. He would put the charge on a ten-minute delay fuse just before leaving the ship. On deck he attached the M60 firing device, taping the igniter to the handrail that he would climb over once the drone launched.

"Hey, guys," he announced to the other three crew engineers on deck. "The firing device is here. I'll set it off once we are in the skiff. Nobody touch it. Okay?"

The men on deck preparing the launch ramp laughed. "Ah c'mon, Del, a nice hot afternoon like this, a swim would feel good," replied one of the men.

Delany smiled and picked up his laptop, checking the GPS coordinates a fifth time. Cross checking the electronic azimuth with the side view blueprint map of the building, he could see that the guidance system would fly the drone literally through the large glass windows and into what looked like a large ballroom of the building. Evidently, this was where everyone to be hit would be in attendance. Confident that the system and the redundancy program were functioning properly, he picked up the secure line SAT phone and punched in the numbers. The phone was answered almost immediately.

"Yes."

Delany looked over at his crew who had started taking the bungee cords off the tarpaulin covering the drone. "Sir, we are now ready. Standing by."

"Copy. We are still monitoring the traffic at the target and will green light when all the players have arrived at the party. Stand by."

"Roger," replied Delany, hanging up the call. "Hey guys, start doing your final preflight. We're getting ready to roll here."

****

Sixty-eight miles away the Bishop, along with twelve handpicked Cardinals, began to make their way through the expansive doors of the main ballroom. De Parman and Costa, along with Sims and several other members of the security unit, stood near the door watching the somber procession of Vatican hierarchy. Costa watched as the Bishop, dressed in period sackcloth, carried a polished rosewood box that he presumed contained all thirteen sets of Medallions. The Cardinals, walking behind, looked like a first century group of over-fed villagers, none of them dressed in the traditional Cardinal red cassock and gold chain Crucifix but wearing the same type of rough sackcloth as the Bishop.

It was truly a bizarre sight as they slowly disappeared inside the stone hut standing in the middle of the great room. On a prearranged signal, the ballroom lights dimmed, the only illumination now coming from the hut's open doorway. A spray of yellow light from the oil lamps spilled out onto the floor as the Bishop inside began the Mass. Costa felt a chill run up his spine as he listened to the men chant the Latin response to the Euclid. There was strange electricity in the air unlike anything Costa had ever felt before in all his years attending Mass. He looked over at De Parman and in the subdued light of the hut saw tears streaming down his face. Something was happening. Costa's emotions, mixed emotions of joy and fear, were now right at the surface. *What if God did answer this attempt to reach Him? What then? How could a man like myself stand before the power of the universe, before God in all His glory?* He was suddenly struck by the wrongness of it all. *This was a mistake.* As the Mass continued, the voices in the hut grew louder, a sign that the participants inside could also feel the rising tension.

"I can't stand this," announced Costa, feeling as if he were about to pass out. "I need some air."

De Parman gave him a confused look. "You're joking?" he whispered. "You're about to witness the greatest event in your lifetime."

"No, really," replied Costa, fighting back the bile. "I'm going to be sick." Sudden nausea rolled through his gut as he quickly stepped away. As fast as he could walk without running, he pushed his way through the large wooden doors at the back of the hall. Holding his mouth, he made it three steps into the hallway before vomiting his dinner onto the polished white marble floor in a violent spray.

****

Seventy miles off the Italian coast, Delany helped the other two engineers pull the cover off the drone. The sun had just set. The lights along the coastline began to sparkle like orange and white jewels in the darkness. Delany checked his wind gauge. "Three knots," he announced to the others. "Nice little tail wind."

"We're ready over here," replied one of the men, removing the locking pins on the drone ramp.

"All right, Steve, go ahead and get in the skiff. Get the engine running. Bob, take the wheelhouse. Turn us into the wind and then shut down everything, all power. I'll launch from my computer. Tim, you're my second set of eyes. I'll be putting this bird in the air in two minutes." He picked up the SAT and punched in the number.

"Yes."

"Sir, we are ready. Fingers on the button." There was a long pause on the other end, long enough for Delany to think that he had lost the connection.

"Sir, sir are you still there?"

"Green light, Mister Delany. You have a GO."

"Yes, sir," he replied, immediately pushing the START sequence button on his laptop. "Bird is inbound in 3-2-1..."

Chapter Thirty-Four

Two floors above the Grand Ballroom, Clark stood at the large set of bedroom windows looking out towards the brightly lit Sistine Chapel several hundred yards away. It really was a magnificent site, even in the dark. Still trying to weigh his options, he had no idea what to expect in the morning when he was to be interrogated by The Committee Intelligence unit. *What limits will they go to if they think I have important information about Stone Gate? How far will they push the issue?* Looking out onto the grounds, he could see that several more cars had arrived at the facility parking lot. Evidently the ceremony downstairs was in full swing. He decided to take a look when curiosity overtook him.

The emotional atmosphere was now at a fever pitch in the main hall where De Parman and the other forty attendees of the ceremony stood transfixed, all eyes locked on the stone hut. Any second now thought the Chairman, rolling the rosary beads through his fingers, it was going to happen. The expectation of a divine manifestation had charged the men in attendance with a heart-pounding sense of fear and joyful expectation, each thinking about their response if the fire and the Spirit actually appeared. All were now confessing past sins, some in whispered gasps, others in silence, desperately searching their hearts for anything that might hinder the holiness of God.

Just as he was about go to his knees in the gallery, De Parman heard the Angel, a sudden roar and a shattering of glass, followed by a thunder clap explosion of bluish white light far more brilliant than anything he had ever seen before. Yet at the microsecond before he died, he knew that this sensation, this intense heat, was all wrong. The thunderous blast lifted him off his feet in a lethal spray of steel and flame. De Parman and the other men in the room were dead before their bodies hit the floor. The men inside the small stone hut conducting the Mass were temporarily shielded from the initial blast, the stones deflecting the shrapnel. But the overpressure and two thousand degree fire flash set every carpet, drape and sackcloth costume in the hall instantly ablaze. The Cardinals and Bishop were now running out of the hut, totally engulfed in flames, their screams of terror and pain echoing throughout the hall.

Clark had just stepped out of his room as the explosion detonated two floors below. Thick smoke and the smell of burning flesh filled the air. As he quickly stumbled down the smoke-filled stairway, he could feel the growing heat of the air. For a second, as he slowly felt his way down the hall to the great room, the thought that maybe God had shown up flashed through his mind, but just as fast he dismissed it. The distinctive smell of military grade explosive hung heavy in the air. No, this was not the ethereal God-directed Holy Spirit blowing in like a mighty wind but something sinister. This was the work of men.

Trying to escape the billowing smoke and growing intensity of the fire, Clark felt his way down the long wide hallway, eventually finding the large front doors and stepping out into the cool night air. The sound of fire engines and ambulance sirens filled the air as Clark collapsed to his knees in the parking lot, trying to catch his breath.

"You all right?" questioned one of the first responders kneeling at his side.

Clark spat on the ground, clearing his throat, "Yeah, yeah I'm fine. What happened?" he asked, slowly getting to his feet.

"Don't know," replied the EMT, guiding him to one of the fire trucks. He sat down on the fender of the truck as the EMT put an oxygen mask on his face. "Just breathe normally. You'll feel better," he announced. "I have to go see other people. Are you sure you're okay?"

"Yeah, I'm fine, go...go."

****

For the rest of the night and well into the next day the bodies of the dead and wounded were taken out of the smoky ruins of the Great Hall. Clark had been moved to the Vatican hospital and treated for mild smoke inhalation. According to the information he was able to gather from the hospital staff, over fifty had been killed with at least a hundred wounded, some critically.

The growing consensus was that it had been a terrorist attack with the attackers still not identified. On the evening of the day after the attack, Clark had just finished getting dressed and was getting ready to leave the hospital. He was now even more confused than ever about his status since his arrival. He had had no visitors, no contact with the Committee Intelligence Unit, and no contact with anyone other than hospital staff. In fact, no one seemed to know him or really have an interest as to what he was doing at the facility. He was treated, asked to sign some release forms, and then told he was free to leave.

Thanking the nurse for her care, he picked up his release paper work and wearing the same clothes he had on the day of the attack, stepped out the hospital's front doors just as the sun was going down.

"Agent Clark."

Clark turned to the voice and saw Costa walking out the doors behind him. "Hello. You survived."

Costa smiled. "Yes, when so many others didn't. How are you doing, Agent? I was just on my way over to see you when they told me that you had been discharged."

"I'm fine." For Clark, the pleasantries had a surreal feeling. They were talking like they were all friends. "Listen, what's going on now? What's my status?"

Costa thought for a moment. "The media is reporting that an Iranian group hostile to the Vatican for it's support of Israel was responsible for the attack. It was an attack carried out using a very sophisticated drone."

"Really, what's the casualty count?"

Costa lit a cigarette, before answering. It was the first time Clark had seen the man smoke. "Fifty-three dead. Seventy injured. The Committee Chairman is among the dead."

"So what happens now?" Clark could see that Costa was still in a disjointed frame of mind, trying to accept the fact that he was still alive.

"You're leaving today."

"Where am I going?"

Costa smiled sadly. "Anywhere you want. The Vatican jet will take you anywhere in the world you wish to go."

"I don't understand. What's going on?"

Costa took a long drag of his cigarette while starring at the ground, his thoughts far away.

"Costa, what's going on? You guys brought me over here. What's next?"

"Two hours after the attack, I was contacted by a person within your intelligence community, someone of great influence. The man told me the attack was from the United States and was a warning to the Committee that we should stop all research considering *Stone Gate*. He said that if we ignored the warning, the Vatican, as we know it, would be destroyed."

"You have got to be kidding me?" replied Clark, still not believing what Costa was saying.

Costa tossed the cigarette butt to the ground looking as if he were about to cry. "I'm not kidding, Mister Clark. I believe him, which is why you are free to leave."

As they started walking down the hospital steps, Clark could see that Costa had a slight limp and in the orange glow of the streetlights could see fear etched deep in his face. The man wasn't sad. He was terrified.

"Sorry that this happened," replied Clark, his mind a blur with questions.

"That's not all the official said, Mister Clark. He specifically asked about you."

"Me?"

"Yes, he wanted to know if you were one of the causalities."

"What did you say?"

"I told him the truth. I said I did not know. It was too early to tell. That is why you have to leave. That strike was also meant for you. They want you dead and will spare no expense in money or blood to see that happen." He handed Clark a soft leather briefcase. "Take it."

"What is this?"

"The two medals that you picked up in the States, along with Robshaw's journal."

"I don't understand," replied Clark taking the case.

"You said something yesterday that struck a chord. You said that maybe the Medallions have been separated all these years for a reason and that maybe they should not be together." Costa waved to a car that was just pulling up to the curb. "Your ride is here."

"I don't understand. Why are you giving me the Medallions?"

Costa walked over and opened the back passenger seat door. "Because I don't want a repeat of what happened last night. It was wrong, and we were punished for it."

"So you believe that there was some kind of divine intervention? God sent the drone?"

Costa motioned for him to get in to the car. "I am a man of faith, Agent Clark. I judge everything that happens in my life as God-directed. This is no different."

Clark walked over and stood in the open door of the car. "And what about *Stone Gate*?"

"That is your government playing God. We no longer will. There will be no more research into the subject. I got the message."

Clark slid into the back seat of the car. "And what am I supposed to do?"

Costa leaned in. "Run, Agent Clark. Run as far away as you can. Powerful men want your head. There is some money waiting for you on the plane - two hundred thousand. It's not much, but it's the best I can do. As I said, give the pilot any destination in the world and he will take you there."

"And the Medallions? Why should I take them? They seem to bring nothing but trouble to whoever has them."

Costa shook his head. "With the kind of people you're dealing with, you will probably need them. Stay alive, Agent Clark," he announced closing the door.

Before Clark could answer, the driver pulled away from the curb. It was over. Nothing else needed to be said. He knew that Costa would only be able to stall the people who had asked about him for a short time. They would want confirmation of his death, and Costa would not lie to cover it. With a force this powerful, the world was a very small place and two hundred thousand dollars when you're on the run is not a tremendous amount of money. It would not last long. Watching the lights of the city flash by on his way to the airport, Clark knew he only had one choice, one chance to stay alive.

He would have to go back to the States, go back and confront the beast that had changed his life so dramatically. He would never be able to run fast enough or far enough to escape. Their reach was too long. His only hope was to face the organization head on and hope that the same kind of divine intervention that Costa believed in would look favorably on him. Seeing the airport lights come into view, Clark found himself praying. Hopefully, God was paying attention.

****

Three days after the drone strike, the investigating authorities had still been unable to figure out where the drone had come from or who really was behind the attack. There was a rumor that the drone came from a fishing trawler some distance off the coast, but no ship had been found. The Iranian government vehemently denied playing any part in the strike as did every terrorist organization from Iraq to Mumby. The media, with its anonymous government sources, continued to feed the story that the Iranians were behind the attack, and despite their protests, they were still painted as the culprits.

***

Braid set the paper down beside his plate of bacon and eggs as the waitress poured his coffee. EJ Briggs, who was sitting on the other side of the table, held up his cup. "Thank you, ma'am, " he said smiling. The men had met at the White Star Café' at eight that morning for breakfast.

"So, I assume we have closed all of our loose ends?" questioned Braid.

"Yes, sir, all except for Agent Clark. We haven't been able to locate him yet. Just a matter of time though."

Braid took a sip of his coffee. "Are we sure he wasn't killed in Rome?"

"Well, that still could be a slim possibility. They are still trying to identify some of the bodies. The fire turned some of those folks into a pile of ash. He may be one of those piles. We are still working on it."

Braid nodded. "All right. Keep me informed on your progress. I won't rest easy until Agent Clark is no longer breathing."

"Yes, sir. If he is alive, we'll find him."

Braid had heard this kind of assuredness before from men who had worked for him over the years. They had been men who honestly believed what they were saying, and most of the time they delivered on the promises. But he knew that when the situation involved desperate men, the outcome would always be in question. Desperate men were reckless and unpredictable which made them dangerous... very dangerous. *Stone Gate* had produced many such desperate men. Some of them were still not accounted for, a thought that had kept him up many a night.

"Use whatever resources you need, E J. I want this ended as quickly as possible."

"Yes, Sir."

****

Six thousand miles away, Clark downed the last of his second beer. He had been on the beach all morning, and now, while waiting for the waiter to bring down his club sandwich and fries, he had the beach to himself. Two days ago he had instructed the pilot of the Vatican jet to drop him off in Bora Bora. They had landed just after midnight at Motu Mute airport, the French Polynesian hub on the island. As he had been told, he had found the small bag of neatly stacked hundred dollar bills on his seat when he boarded the jet and had been assured by the pilot that he would not be bothered at any customs terminal anywhere outside the United States. He had been handed a diplomatic ID card with a Vatican seal embossed on the front along with his picture. Costa had really come through.

After landing, he had caught a cab and asked the driver to take him to the Saint Regis Hotel. A lifetime ago, he had spent two glorious weeks there with his wife. It had been a time of morning swims in the warm brilliant blue water of the lagoon and passionate love making in the afternoon. They had been married for years by that time but there was something about the tropical atmosphere that aroused them as if they had been teenagers. Over those two weeks, they had fallen in love all over again.

Now he was back, back in the only place he truly felt safe. He knew that this peace would be short lived. The hotel had let him pay cash, and he had registered under a different name. He had already made several inquires for a ship to leave on. It was amazing what kind of space and peace real money could buy. Still, as determined as the *Stone Gate* people were in protecting their project, it was just a matter of time before they figured out that his remains were not in the burned out rubble back in Rome. They would come looking for him.

However for the moment, this very minute, he sat back in his chair with his bare feet in the warm sand, a cold beer in hand, and looked out into the azure blue water, remembering better days. He could almost hear his wife calling him from the bungalow, telling him she wanted him…needed his body. He always smiled at the memory of his wife, a woman raised in a Southern Baptist home, shouting racy comments. Because it was not her usual style to be so blunt, it had been sexy and funny at the same time. God, he missed her, missed her more than anything in the world.

He had vowed to her that they would come back and walk on the sand, maybe even renew their vows, but a year to the day after they had arrived back home in Albuquerque, his wife of fourteen years died of a brain aneurysm while she was washing their dog in the bathroom. He had come home that night after five and found their five-year-old German Shepherd, Max, still sitting in now cold bath water shivering, Patty's lifeless body slumped over the side. Max would not leave her. He was her protector, even in death.

A minute later, a deeply tanned Polynesian waiter walked up smiling, "I have your lunch, sir," he announced setting the tray down on the small table. "Would you like another beer, sir?"

Clark nodded, taking the metal lid off the sandwich. "You bet, in fact I'll take two more. Gonna be out here the rest of the afternoon."

"Very good, sir. I'll be right back."

Hardship and loss had been a theme that had been running through his life ever since Patty died. It was as if she had been the glue that had held everything together. As he ate, he wondered what she would say now, what advice would she give? They had had countless discussions over the course of their marriage about his career, talking about options, ideas, where to go, what to do, and always, without fail, she would be spot-on with her advice. It had been one of the million things he loved about her.

He smiled knowing exactly what she would say. When that little southern gal got mad, not angry, but really mad, her eyes would narrow, and with her shoulders back, rising to her full five-foot two inches, she would look you right in the eye and let it rip. He knew she would look him in the eye at this time and tell him to not back down, to swing for the fence, to go on the offensive.

He knew he would be going after *Stone Gate* and finish what had been started in New Mexico. He had the Medallions. Maybe that would give him an edge. That's what his Patty would tell him to do, and she would keep saying it until he had the drive to hit back. With tears in his eyes, he raised his beer. "Here's to you, sweetheart," he whispered. "I'll always love you, and, baby, I hear you. I hear you loud and clear."

Epilogue

Agent Stacy quietly waited as Braid finished the After Action Report or AAR from the Vatican attack. He had arrived in the supervisor's office early that morning, having been summoned from home just after six in the morning.

"So, we are sure Clark is not among the dead?" questioned Braid sitting back in his chair.

"That's correct, sir. It's taken them the last five days to get the forensic team to identify everyone. Clark is not there."

Braid sipped his coffee thinking. "Five days, he could be anywhere by now," he said, thinking out loud.

"Sir, I understand that Rodriquez had breached National Security and deserved elimination but I have a question about Clark."

"And what question would that be?"

"Well, sir, aside from Clark getting on an airplane, what has he really done to get our attention?"

"Are you questioning the importance of the decisions this office is making, Agent Stacy?"

"No, sir. It's just that I was wondering if there was something I was missing."

Braid sipped his coffee again. "Are you familiar with what *Stone Gate* really is?" he asked flatly.

"Most of it. I've not been read into all of it."

"When Professor Taylor's lab exploded and burned to the ground in Albuquerque two years ago, the anomaly was exposed. It created a split in the space-time continuum ten feet long by five feet wide in the pit where Taylor's lab had stood. Clark, who had been searching for one of the missing scientists involved with the Professor was the first person on the scene after the explosion and fire."

"Jesus, I had no idea."

"Well, the problem we have with Agent Clark, is that he has been affected by his encounter with the Anomaly."

"Affected, affected how?"

Braid shook his head. "After studying this thing for two years, our people have discovered that when someone has had close contact with the anomaly, they are now somehow connected with the thing. It draws them. There is some level of pull on the subconsciousness, pulling them to it. Clark was held at a rendering facility for two weeks in an attempt to break this hold. The reeducation has failed."

Stacy was amazed at his supervisor's candor. "Which means what?"

Braid smiled without humor. "Which means, Agent Stacy, that he will be coming our way, drawn by a force he does not understand. He will be seeking something that he must not be allowed to find."

"Sir, if he is coming after *Stone Gate*, why don't we let him? Saves us the trouble of hunting him down?"

Stacy watched as a strange combination of fear and confusion flashed across Braid's face, a fleeting glimpse of something the supervisor kept buried, probably for some time. "It's not that easy. We've tried that, twice, and it does not stop him."

Stacy shook his head. 'Sir, I'm confused, what do you mean we have tried it twice."

Braid eased back into his chair with a sigh, obviously wrestling with some emotional weight. "Stone Gate is a project that allows us to move through the space time continuum. We have run two complete scenarios, and Agent Clark survives each time and we don't know why."

Stacy's head was spinning. "Ah, I'm not following you, sir. What do you mean that you have run two other scenarios?"

Braid leaned forward on his desk. "It means that you and I have had this same conversation before. We have discussed this same problem before. Clark cannot be killed. It's like he has some kind of strange power that makes it impossible to eliminate him. This will be the third time we have done this. This time I want it to end."

"Sir, are you saying that we have repeated history twice before and this is still a problem? I mean, I ..ah, I'm not sure what to say. It sounds unbelievable."

Braid nodded. "That's the capability we have with *Stone Gate*. We can change history, all history except what pertains to Agent Clark, and we need to know why. This has to be answered before the project can move on."

Stacy fought to control his emotions as a million questions raced through his head. "Sir, if Clark is finally eliminated, what will *Stone Gate* change?"

"Everything," whispered Braid. "Everything."

End of Book Two.

Acknowledgements

I want to thank Terri and Linda for the tremendous work and effort with this book. Without them it would not be possible.

71148546R00140

Made in the USA
Columbia, SC
25 May 2017